On Christmas Tree Cove

On Christmas Tree Cove

Sarah Vance-Tompkins

With love,
Sarah
xoxo

TULE
PUBLISHING

Dedication

For everyone who loves sparkling snowflakes and twinkling lights but believes true love and acts of kindness are the real Christmas magic.

Acknowledgments

I am grateful to Jane Porter and Meghan Farrell for asking me to write a Christmas romance. It's been a dream come true. Thank you so much to Julie Sturgeon, my very patient editor, and the Tule design team for creating the most beautiful cover ever. And thanks to everyone else at Tule Publishing, especially Nikki Babri.

Every morning I join the SMUT U writers collective to put crank out words for two hours. I couldn't make it through a day without the support of Sam Tschida, Jennifer Kirkeby, Amanda Wilson, Rainey Dahm, Joe White, Larissa Zageris, Sydney Telcontar, Dara Dokas, Jeanine Coulombe, Jenna O'Brien, and Virginia Brasch. I am also grateful for feedback and encouragement from Barbara Ankrum and Susannah Erwin on Thursday nights.

Separated by an ocean but united by K-dramas and a shared birthplace, Sarah Karabelski scraped me up off the floor and set me back on the right path more times than I can count. You have my eternal love and devotion.

My mom has always been my biggest fan. She fell in love with northern Michigan in 1958. My dad loved books. It's no wonder I had to tell a story in the north woods. They are both forever in my heart. Every year at Christmas my only wish is to wake up next to Kevin Tompkins for the rest of my life. You will always be the frosting on my cupcake. xo

Prologue

Christmas Eve

CHRISTMAS TREE COVE looked like a snow globe right after it had been shaken. Morgan Adair couldn't have cared less. Pushing through the front door of Hillcrest House, she dropped her keys into the green ceramic bowl on the antique wooden table by the front door, pausing for a moment to consider the little dish that served as the messy depository. On any other day, she wouldn't have spared a second glance at her mother's spare keys or her father's tugboat key. They were innocuous bits of flotsam and jetsam in the busy life of the Adair family. But tonight, the keys nearly shredded her heart. She leaned against the door and took a deep, ragged breath.

The Alexa on the coffee table in the living room was still on, playing a soundtrack of Christmas classics her dad always hummed under his breath this time of year. Brightly wrapped packages had been placed in the space under an enormous Christmas tree in the front window. Her mom had so lovingly spent an evening right after Thanksgiving covering the tree in lights and filling its branches with ornaments, both new and heirloom.

Three nights ago, Dad had carefully laid the logs for a Christmas Eve fire. He'd carried the wood into the house in a canvas satchel, taking care to build a log pile with kindling on the bottom and finishing with beautiful, paper-skinned birch logs on the top.

Six fully stuffed stockings were hung from the mantle at perfectly measured intervals. Morgan, her brother, and their two sisters were all old enough to know the truth about Santa, but they still looked forward to opening stockings on Christmas Eve after church.

Morgan's heart squeezed.

Christmas at Hillcrest House was canceled.

The stockings would be ignored. The presents would go unnoticed for weeks, before being unwrapped and unceremoniously returned to the stores. All of the preparations. All of the decorations. None of them would be appreciated. In the blink of an eye, her family's lives, and the holiday, had been forever altered.

It was as if she was attempting to walk through gelatin. Every step took so much effort.

Four hours ago.

Had it only been four hours? The casserole she'd been preparing was on the counter, still waiting to be put in the oven. The cheese on top was congealed and hard. The Christmas pie she'd taken out of the pie safe had fallen, and the whipped cream had separated. Everything needed to be cleaned and put away, but it was too overwhelming a task to face.

She turned back into the dining room. Her heart skipped a beat. She'd been standing in exactly the same spot four hours earlier when the sheriff said her parents were dead.

Morgan's legs could no longer support the weight of her body. She dropped to the floor. Wrapping her arms around her knees, she rocked back and forth, fighting to hold back tears.

When she finally wore herself out, her feet were burning with wet cold. She hurried up the curving staircase to the second floor, down the long hall, and up the cramped wooden steps into her teenage lair to change her jeans and socks before Eli and her sisters came home.

Be strong.

She kicked off her jeans, picked a dry pair off the floor, and pulled them on. She fumbled in a dresser drawer for a clean pair of socks, then sat down in the window seat of the tower room's nook to discard her clammy socks.

Her tower bedroom was the only room on the third floor and the smallest in the house, but it had the best view of the harbor in all of Christmas Tree Cove. The windows were streaked with ice and snow, but colored lights in the harbor, sparkling and reflecting off the water, drew her eye. She pressed her face against the glass to see if her eyes were playing tricks on her.

No. She could see it. An evergreen tree, covered in

brightly colored lights with a golden star at the top, was floating in a small dinghy on Christmas Tree Cove. Her heart skipped a beat.

It was her favorite Christmas tradition. One she shared with her mom. Morgan closed her eyes as memories of Christmas past washed over her. Wrapped up in warm blankets and homemade patchwork quilts on this window seat when she was a little girl, Morgan and her mom would keep an eye out for Santa in the night sky.

When Morgan was more grown up, she counted on spending those magical moments on Christmas Eve with her mom—just the two of them—looking out over their beloved cove before the chaos of Christmas morning.

Mom would make hot cocoa and buttered popcorn as a midnight snack. Snuggled together when everyone else was already in bed, they'd wrap their hands around steaming mugs to keep their fingers warm when the cold lake air rattled the windows.

The lighted tree in the harbor symbolized everything Morgan loved about holiday celebrations in Christmas Tree Cove. She closed her eyes. If only she could turn back time . . . if only for a few hours. Then she stopped herself.

"You can't go back," she said out loud.

She still needed to tell Eli, Dacey, and Kayla what had happened. She needed to put her emotions away for safe-keeping, like Mom always did with her baked goods in the pie safe in the kitchen. Morgan took a deep breath.

Staring at the Christmas tree in the harbor, she touched her fingers to her lips, bringing back the memories of the sweet kisses she'd shared with Jesse Taylor that afternoon in Fish Village. The promises they'd made.

Six hours ago.

In the freezing rain on the bench behind Obermeyer's shanty, she and Jesse had made a commitment to build a life together. He'd been accepted to the graduate program at the School of the Art Institute of Chicago, and she'd secured tuition reimbursement from a major airline for the ATP pilot training program. They'd found an apartment and planned to tell their parents they were going to live together.

"Maybe we should tell them we're only friends," she suggested. "Slowly ease them into the idea of a romantic relationship."

Jesse shook his head. "We're not kids. They can't be surprised that we're in love. They'll probably be glad that we have each other in Chicago rather than going it alone."

"You want to tell my dad we're dating? Are you crazy?"

"Point well taken." He'd pushed his glasses up his nose and brushed his fingers through his dark curls in one sweeping motion. "Despite the fact that your dad may kick my ass from here to tomorrow, we should tell them. No matter the consequences. We've been keeping us a secret for too long."

Morgan nodded and leaned her head on Jesse's shoulder. Her breath hitched.

"What do you love more? All the twinkling stars scattered across the midwinter sky? Or the lights reflected on the water from the tree on Christmas Tree Cove?"

Jesse's answer never changed. And he never hesitated. Which both thrilled and frightened her.

Morgan shook her head to come back to the present.

She'd have to break her promise to him. Jesse would be hurt, but it didn't matter. Nothing mattered anymore. Eventually, he'd forget her and move on. She needed to focus on keeping her family together.

"Hey! Is anyone home?" Eli shouted.

A few seconds later the tinkling brightness of her sister Kayla's voice joined his and stabbed Morgan through her already broken heart. She was going to be the one to tell them the truth.

"What's going on? Where is Morgan?" Dacey demanded. Her siblings were home.

"Dunno." Eli's response was more grunt than words.

"She hasn't gotten around to setting the table yet?" It was Kayla. She must be in the dining room. "Where is she? What has she been doing? The casserole isn't in the oven either."

"Turn on the oven and help me set the table," Dacey said with a sweet giggle. Morgan could hear the metal sound of silverware being handled. "Can you light the fire, Eli?"

Their lives had changed. They didn't know it yet.

Be strong.

She took a deep breath. She would be a rock for her brother and sisters. An unmovable force that they'd have in their corner, no matter what obstacles were thrown in their path. Morgan bit her lower lip, casting one last wistful glance back at the lighted tree floating in the waves in the harbor. Then she left the comfort of her tower bedroom and went downstairs.

Chapter One

Six years later

"YOU'RE MAKING ME believe in love at first sight."

Taking her aviator sunglasses from the pocket of her Carhartt overalls, Morgan covered the yearning in her dark-green eyes.

"Nah. I'm not that easy." She shook her head, flashing a tight smile for emphasis. She'd use up her last breath denying it, but the truth was, Morgan had fallen hard for the large shiny object parked on the tarmac in front of the fixed-based operator headquarters in the winter sunshine. The brand-new Gulfstream executive jet could seat up to eleven passengers and carry enough fuel for over nine hours of flying time.

She shoved her hands deeper into the pockets of her overalls and turned her back against knife-sharp wind cutting across the airport from Lake Michigan. For one blissful moment, Morgan allowed herself to believe she could get out in front of all her problems if only she were the pilot of this jet.

"Don't lie to me, girl," Skip Brunell said, rubbing a bear's paw-size hand over the close-cropped white hair on his head and grizzled chin. The owner of Northwoods Aviation, he'd been Morgan's boss for the past five years, but he'd known her all her life. She might be able to fool herself, but she wasn't able to fool him. "You've got it bad."

Morgan grinned. Maybe it was best to admit failure. Hiding her feelings from Skip was a lost cause.

Growing up, Morgan loved Barbie, Palomino ponies, and anything that went fast—not necessarily in that order. Her need for speed started with bikes, graduated to cars and boats, and quickly jumped to things not required to stay on the ground. All of her teenage dreams had been about flying jets and going places like Norway, Portugal, and the Maldives. When she wasn't at cheerleading or volleyball practice, she was in the career counseling office making plans to become a commercial airline pilot.

Then her parents died, and she'd re-prioritized her life. Eli finished his degree at the University of Michigan with honors. Dacey went to Yale for business school. And Kayla had been the prom queen and was now the art teacher at the elementary school. She was so proud of all they'd accomplished. Her parents would be too.

"If you went to the pilot training program and got checked out on this jet, you wouldn't have to take on crappy, part-time jobs to make ends meet during the winter months," Skip suggested, coaxing her in a gentle tone. It was difficult to ignore his logic.

When she wasn't ferrying hunters and fishermen into

remote locations along northern Lake Michigan between January and April, she had a tough time paying bills. She'd learned to live on a budget, but every year her money didn't seem to go as far. She'd never admit it to anyone, but she was drowning in debt, and Hillcrest House needed significant repairs she'd never be able to afford.

You're in trouble.

Her heart started to race. She gulped cold, crisp air, trying to prevent a full-blown panic attack. She didn't have time to deal with her dark feelings. Especially not today. She stuffed them away.

Be strong.

"Yes, but the Kimuras count on me to work at Forget-Me-Not Flowers when I'm not flying in the winter. I can't imagine this year will be any different," she said. The part-time gig didn't pay much, but it helped. Without the Kimuras, she'd have to make significant changes to her very frugal lifestyle.

"You could fly for me full time, year 'round," Skip suggested. "Or once you qualified, you could work for a major airline. You could go anywhere in the world."

Morgan's heart was thudding in her chest. All she'd ever dreamed about was being dangled like a carrot in front of her. If only life was that easy.

Be happy with what you have.

Keeping a placid smile on her face, Morgan stuffed her feelings into the dark space—the pie safe—where she kept them hidden away until they cooled. "I appreciate your confidence, Skip, I do, but I'm fine."

Your life is fine. As is.

"Are you sure?" Skip wasn't giving up without a fight. "The de Havilland Beaver you fly every day was built in 1967. It's an antique—basically a vintage Ford F-150," Skip said, ducking under the wing to follow Morgan on her close-up inspection of the new executive jet. "And this…this is a brand-new Lamborghini."

"The Beaver is fine by me," Morgan countered. She took a step back from the jet, picked up her flight bag, and continued on a direct path through all the airplanes and airport equipment on the apron. "It may be a workhorse, but so am I."

"What's your ceiling in the Beaver?" Skip challenged, following along behind her.

Morgan stiffened. What would it take to make him give up?

She sighed before she answered with a tight smile. "Five hundred feet."

"In the jet, you'll be above five hundred feet in less than thirty seconds." Skip crossed his arms over his chest. "You could soar, Morgan Adair."

Be brave.

Morgan stopped and took a breath. Her heart was fluttering. No matter what Skip said, she wasn't going to take the bait. Not today. Not when Eli and Dacey were coming home, and the sky was azure blue, dotted with white, cotton ball clouds.

"Seriously. I'm good." She put a hand up to stop any more discussion of her dream of flying jets. Skip had good intentions, but her patience was at an end.

After her parents were killed, he'd given her a semiperm-anent job and become a loyal ally. She didn't doubt him. "In the de Havilland, you're nothing but a bush pilot, Morgan," Skip said, delivering the final blow in his pitch.

Morgan raised an eyebrow, no longer able to hide her rising ire. "*Nothing but* a bush pilot?"

"Don't get me wrong," Skip backpedaled. "I don't know any other pilot who can land a plane built like a middle linebacker as if she's a prima ballerina in toe shoes. Especially on moving water. You're the best I've ever seen," he defend-ed himself. It was the truth. Morgan was an excellent pilot.

"My dad had a rule about mooring boats and planes," she said. "Never approach a dock any faster than you want to hit it."

Skip laughed ruefully. "Okay. I won't push you."

"Thanks," she said. "And for letting me fly the three-thirteen."

"I'm glad the Adair clan will be back together for Thanksgiving."

"First time since the accident we'll all be around the table for a holiday," she said with a bright smile. Everyone would have a good time, and she'd find the piece of her heart she'd been missing for six years.

"When was the last time Eli was home?" Skip asked.

"It's been more than a year." Morgan beamed. "Dacey hasn't been home in a year and a half." Her brother was the only passenger scheduled on the brief afternoon flight. Dacey was driving up from Chicago. "I'm going to fly up over Northport, buzz the Stony Point lighthouse, and take a low pass out over the coastal islands."

"Christmas Tree Cove will be a glittering winter wonderland," Skip agreed.

"A bird's-eye view of the harbor in the winter is my favorite." She nodded. If she timed it right, they'd be landing in the harbor at sunset. She hoped they'd be gifted with magical winter light when streaks of orange, gold, and pink reflected off the water and set the entire sky on fire. They'd be late for their estimated arrival at three-thirteen, but she doubted Eli would complain.

Morgan grabbed a clipboard and started the preflight on the Cessna 206. The tiny plane had been fitted with both floats and wheels to fly a regular route between Cherry Capital Airport in Traverse City and the harbor in Christmas Tree Cove.

Tossing her thick braid of mahogany hair over her shoulder, she ducked under the tail to inspect the airworthiness of the plane. She was on her hands and knees when someone shouted.

"Hey! You know where the pilot for the three-thirteen

is?"

Morgan backed out from under the plane, bottom first. Crawling out on the frozen tarmac, she nearly swallowed her tongue when she came face-to-face with him . . . the last man on earth she wanted to see. His name tumbled off her lips with a bitter grimace.

"Jesse Taylor."

The man who'd gotten past all of her roadblocks. The man who made her feel things like complete joy and utter despair.

"Morgan Adair," he immediately responded. Speaking her name as if accusing her of a crime, yet the sound of his voice made her already racing heart skip a beat.

Reveal nothing. Don't show pain.

She hadn't seen Jesse in a long time. At least not up close. After graduating from the Art Institute of Chicago, he'd moved to New York City. She'd been unable to avoid tales of his success as an in-demand commercial photographer. Sure, she'd caught a glimpse of him now and then when he visited Christmas Tree Cove. Down the street. Across a crowded restaurant. On the other side of the docks in the harbor. But she never went near Fish Village. And they hadn't spoken. Well, not since that night when her entire world crumbled.

Be brave.

She hoped her mirrored aviators were doing their job. It was hard to gauge. Especially when her pulse had dropped a beat. One. Two. Cha-cha-cha. The pounding rhythm of her heart kept her from doing anything other than staring up at him.

Jesse was impossibly tall, but then he'd always been long and very lean. Despite his height, in elementary school he was the most likely to be picked last in dodgeball. He didn't play football with the rest of the boys under the lights on Friday nights in high school either. He read poetry and wore an old Leica camera around his neck on a leather strap. He was an oddity in Christmas Tree Cove. He didn't care if he didn't fit in. That's what she'd liked about him the most.

Morgan swallowed hard.

He wore his hair long, his black curls tamed by product. Dressed in a cashmere sweater, expensive wool pants, and leather driving mocs, Jesse had seriously glowed up over the past six years. The epitome of urbane masculine elegance, he looked more like a fashion model than a photographer who was more appropriately attired for attendance at the Concours d'Elegance on the Monterrey Peninsula than flying a pontoon plane into a small harbor in northern Michigan.

Someone had styled him—a woman, no doubt.

Whoever she was, she had taken the edge off the awkward geek that had always been the essence of Jesse's personality. A spark of jealousy ignited in the pit of Morgan's stomach. She closed her eyes, willing the emotions she didn't want to go away.

It almost worked until she noticed the woman following

Jesse across the tarmac.

Grace Cunningham, the most popular girl in high school. They'd been on cheer together. She'd glammed up into the kind of woman who could make chunky L.L. Bean catalogue clothes look sexy as hell. Of course she had. And Jesse and Grace made a perfect-looking pair.

Stop. Stop it now.

Morgan returned her focus to Jesse's face. He'd given up the oblong, wire-rimmed glasses that weren't strong enough to hold lenses as thick as his prescription required, and thus were always bent and held together with cellophane tape. He'd traded them in for an expensive-looking pair of dark-rimmed frames. His blue eyes were as intense as ever. She could only maintain eye contact with him for a few seconds.

Honestly, he looked like Clark Kent. No. He looked better. He looked like Superman. Which was bad news for Morgan since Jesse Taylor had always been her kryptonite.

Chapter Two

"THE THREE-THIRTEEN TO Christmas Tree Cove," Jesse prompted again. "Where's the pilot?" Jesse scraped a hand through his thick black curls, hoping to calm his anxiety.

"You're looking at her." Morgan wrinkled her nose and grinned up at him.

"Wait. No. Where's Skip?" Jesse asked. His eyes glanced over the tarmac as a cold knot formed in the pit of his stomach. Skip always piloted the afternoon flight to Christmas Tree Cove. It was something a nervous flyer like Jesse counted on. Despite his better judgment, the blustery old bastard had convinced him the seaplane that landed in the harbor four times a day was the safest way to travel on the last leg of his frequent travels to and from Christmas Tree Cove.

"I traded with Skip for this flight. He's dropping a group of hunters up at Shadow Creek for me." Morgan's voice was sharp.

"Why? Why would he do that?" Jesse shook his head. He'd been double-crossed.

"Because I asked him," she snapped. "Eli is coming home for Thanksgiving. I wanted to be the one to fly him home."

Jesse leaned in awkwardly, jamming both his hands deep into his pockets. His tone gentled. "Is this the first time since . . .?"

His voice trailed off. Morgan had always been guarded about her feelings, but after her parents died, she'd completely shut down. She was emotionless as a cyborg. A really beautiful cyborg. He was still angry at her dismissal of him, but compassionate enough not to push her too far. She looked so fragile.

"What are you doing here?" Morgan demanded. "Your name isn't on the passenger manifest."

He wrinkled his brow. "Skip knew I was on this flight," Jesse insisted. "I texted him yesterday."

Why did his pilot have to be Morgan Adair?

She loved to fly. He hated it. This was going to be so awkward. Especially if he was afflicted with motion sickness. He had a sinking feeling in his stomach. Before his anxiety had a chance to get the best of him, he was distracted by a call from Matt Wendell, who worked for a prestigious magazine group that frequently hired him for well-paying jobs. Jesse hit answer before the second ring.

"Have I got an offer for you," Matt said. "What would you say if I told you I could hand you your dream job?"

Jesse laughed, his eyes briefly falling on Morgan. "I'm glad someone knows exactly what I want."

"Editorial control. And a steady paycheck. No more fighting for freelance contracts."

Jesse had no idea he was so transparent. And yet the truth was more complicated. He was caught between the allure of financial success in New York City and wanting to return to the comforts of Christmas Tree Cove, where he'd left his heart so long ago. And here he was standing next to a very small plane, looking at the woman who'd broken it.

"Listen. I'm headed home for Thanksgiving and about to get on a very small plane. Can I call you back when we land?"

"No problem," Matt said. "Call me when you get a chance."

Jesse clicked off and turned to face Morgan. She was still achingly beautiful, although her natural beauty was more difficult to see since she'd been carrying the weight of the world on her shoulders for six years. Her brow was furrowed. Her smile was studied and forced. On the tarmac of an airport, her cheeks were pink with cold, making the tiny freckles sprinkled across her nose stand out against her pale, porcelain skin. Morgan looked like a rose that had bloomed after the first frost, wilting before it ever had a chance to fully blossom.

Before her parents were killed, Morgan had lived life unafraid of consequences. She never backed down from a fight.

Growing up in Christmas Tree Cove as the tall, skinny kid who liked to listen to music and read poetry had been a living nightmare, and blunt-talking Morgan had come to his rescue on more than one occasion. Despite her small stature, she didn't scare easy.

She'd been his crush, his biggest defender against bullies—his best friend. He'd fallen head over heels in love with her. And she with him. Then she'd broken his heart. Despite all that, he still measured every woman he met against her.

She was waving her hand in front of his face. "Are you okay?"

"I'm fine."

"You sure?" She squinted into his face, as if trying to assess his current state of mind. "You drifted off for a second." A smile played on her lips. She was enjoying this.

"I'm fine," he said, though he clearly wasn't. "As long as you can accommodate all of us."

"All?"

"Me and Grace." He nodded toward the main terminal where his baby sister, Aurora, was dragging a rolling suitcase behind her. "And Aurora's on her way too."

"No problem. I can add you guys to the manifest before I go into the office to get my flight plan stamped."

"Hey, Aurora! How much do you weigh?" Morgan asked without any preamble or apology.

"Can I tell you how tall I am instead?" Aurora sassed. She'd always been a princess.

Morgan raised an eyebrow. "It's not about you. It's about weight distribution."

Aurora remained silent, with her arms crossed over her chest. Jesse shook his head. His baby sister had the same attitude as Morgan.

"If you don't tell me, I'll be forced to guesstimate."

"Fine by me." Aurora threw up her hands.

"Rory," Jesse admonished. "Be nice to our pilot."

Pushing her sunglasses up the bridge of her nose, Morgan considered the young woman over the top of her clipboard, then wrote down a number. Aurora looked over her shoulder at the note. "One-fifty. As if."

"Okay. Can I see some identification?" Morgan asked Grace with a polite smile.

Grace was more familiar with the pre-boarding questions for the small plane. She handed over her driver's license without complaint, and Morgan wrote down her information.

"Is this how they identify the bodies after we crash?" Aurora challenged, looking at her brother. "You said flying to Christmas Tree Cove is safer than driving."

"It is." Morgan and Jesse jinxed each other by answering at the same time.

"We're not going to crash," Morgan said. She forced a flat smile that didn't reach her eyes. It was, no doubt, something she'd practiced so clients who tried to get too friendly would keep their distance.

"Will you need help stowing your bags?" she asked.

Jesse squared his shoulders. "*That* I can handle."

He opened the luggage compartment, forcing himself to focus on loading the metal suitcases that held his photographic equipment, and not the aircraft's pilot. Grace and Aurora settled themselves while Morgan inspected the lights on one of the wings.

But then something made her take a step back.

"Huh," she said.

"What?" Jesse dropped Aurora's bag and joined Morgan near the wing of the plane. "What is that supposed to mean? Is everything all right?" he stuttered as his heartbeat quickened.

Morgan sucked in her cheeks. "It's nothing. Everything'll be fine."

"What do you mean, 'everything'll be fine'?" He was quickly moving into panic mode, which was not a good look on him. Not in front of Morgan. Not after all this time.

She turned to him with one hand on her hip. "Let me ask you a question, Jesse. Have you ever seen *The Sound of Music*?"

He rolled his eyes. "Julie Andrews. Christopher Plummer. A house full of kids. And Nazis. My mom makes us watch it every year at Christmas."

Morgan smiled. "Do you remember how Maria sings about her favorite things to feel better during a thunderstorm?"

He shook his head. "Kinda. Maybe I should've paid better attention."

"Well, if this were *The Sound of Music* and I was going to sing about my favorite things, every note in my song would be about flying this plane." Her tone softened to a soothing lilt. "Nothing's wrong with the plane. I promise. And I'm a really good pilot."

Then she ducked under the wing to march across to the FBO to file the manifest and get her flight plan stamped. Jesse laughed, loud and long. Seeing a flash of swagger and bravado on Morgan's face gave him a bit of hope, reminding him of the girl he once loved.

Just then an expensive sports car pulled into the parking and a man with shaggy brown hair unfurled himself from behind the steering wheel. Morgan stepped back onto the tarmac from the Northwoods Aviation building. The guy sent a scornful look in her direction.

"Morgan-a," he shouted. "Is that my witchy sister, Morgan-a?"

"Eli!" Morgan waved.

Jesse covered his mouth so she wouldn't see him laughing.

Eli had always added an "a" at the end of her name. He claimed it was on her birth certificate. It wasn't. He did it to irritate her. And it always worked. "I'm relieved to find out we'll be flying into Christmas Tree Cove on something other than a broom."

Eli ducked out of the way of Morgan's playful pat. Jesse crossed his arms over his chest and smiled broadly at the unfolding Adair family reunion. Eli tossed his backpack over one shoulder and walked to the plane. He stopped when he recognized Jesse.

"Jesse? Jesse Taylor, is that you?" Eli greeted him with a broad smile. Glib and easygoing, Eli had always been the most gregarious of the Adair family. "Hey, Aurora," he added. "I haven't seen you in forever."

Jesse grinned and shook Eli's hand. "It's been a long time. I understand you've finally found a way to make money slacking off and swilling beer."

"We started with one artisanal brewery in Ann Arbor," Eli said with passion and enthusiasm. "Now we've got three different pub locations and distribution throughout the Midwest."

Eli dropped his gear near Morgan's feet as Grace and Aurora were settling into forward seats.

Jesse hung out near the tarmac, hoping for a miracle so he wouldn't have to get on the tiny plane to Christmas Tree Cove. He supervised Eli tossing his bag into the luggage compartment.

"Hey, Eli," Morgan called. "Can you ride in the backseat and do your 'appliance-salesman thing' on Jesse? He's not an easy flier."

"I beg your pardon," Jesse said.

"Look at you," Morgan said. "You're getting ready to ask me if we can drive the plane out to the coast."

His outlook brightened momentarily. "Is that possible?"

he asked.

Eli raised an eyebrow. "Don't get too upset. She's misidentifying my marketing skills in favor of a less-than-stellar assessment of my personality." Jesse laughed, letting go of some of the tension he'd been feeling. He slid into the seat directly behind the cockpit.

Eli squared his shoulders and saluted his sister. "Aye, aye, Captain, my captain. Your wish is my command." He hopped into the seat next to Jesse and opened his iPad. "How does a virtual tour of our new brewery operations sound?"

Jesse grinned. Six years after she'd pushed him away without offering an explanation, Morgan was still protecting him. "Sounds like a ploy to keep me from noticing that we're five hundred feet above ground without a safety net," he said.

Eli grimaced. "Don't be insulted. Morgan-a just said I remind her of an appliance salesman."

Morgan was too busy talking to the tower to defend herself. While waiting for runway clearance, she did a run up of the engines. That's when Jesse's stomach dropped. "Hey. I can see through the fuselage," he said, pointing to a place where two pieces of metal no longer came together.

Morgan dismissed his concerns without a glance. "That? That's nothing," she said. "It's been there since we were in high school."

"Seriously?" Jesse glanced in Eli's direction for support.

Eli recoiled a bit at the sight. "I don't know, Morgan-a," Eli said. "I can definitely see sky through the gap."

"All right," Morgan said. "I'll take a look at it. Later. But right now, you both need to hang on."

"Why?" Jesse said.

Air traffic control answered. "Runway twenty-two, you've been cleared for takeoff."

"Roger, TVC Air Center, I'm northwest bound." She pulled back on the throttle and the engines immediately responded.

Jesse focused on keeping his breathing even and regular. He pressed his forehead against the cold glass window next to the hole in the fuselage, willing himself not to succumb to motion sickness. Not today. Not in front of Morgan.

THE WINTER SUN was beginning to dip lower into the horizon. The moving reflection of the airplane cast a shadow on the ground far below that looked like a Christmas quilt handmade by Mother Nature.

Keeping his gaze on the Stony Point Lighthouse and the residential neighborhoods lining the shore on the south side of the cove, Jesse willed himself to enjoy the spectacular view. All of a sudden, Lake Michigan appeared, never-ending and sparkling crystalline-blue, next to the pure-white, snow-dusted terrain.

Jesse put the viewfinder of his camera between himself and the ground so far below, taking comfort in the routine feeling of snapping photographs. He was content for a few minutes. Then, without warning, the plane dropped. Eli let go of a long, low whistle.

"Are we landing?" he asked.

Morgan nodded. "Hang on."

First Jesse's seat fell out from underneath him—then his stomach. The two caught up to each other at a lower altitude, giving him the sensation of weighing a literal ton.

"Landing on Christmas Tree Cove is always a bit of a squealer." Morgan grinned. "The air gets rough near the shore."

She wasn't lying. The plane buffeted wildly in the wind over the harbor. Jesse was certain he was going to be sick.

Jesse focused on the glittery snow-dusted earth rising to meet the plane. Then the nose of the plane dipped, and the sparkling snow gave way to the dark blue water, growing ever closer as the nose of the plane pointed directly down at Lake Michigan.

Jesse dug his fingers into the seat until his nails were white. He closed his eyes. The plane's floats touched down on the water with an unexpectedly hard jolt.

"Whoa," Aurora said, her eyes wide with excitement. She smiled up at Grace.

"Big hit of adrenaline," Eli laughed.

Skidding across the waves, the plane came to a slow and

gradual floating stop.

"Welcome to Christmas Tree Cove," Morgan said, steering the plane around in a wide U-turn. The plane motored back through the breakwater into the harbor.

Jesse let go of the breath he'd been holding. He forced a smile, but didn't say a word. If he opened his mouth to speak, he might squeak like a Christmas mouse.

Chapter Three

Thanksgiving

ORGAN TRUDGED UP the hill, returning from the mercantile with a few odds and ends for Thanksgiving dinner in her shopping bags, as well as Eli's favorite breakfast cereal and the pumpkin muffins Dacey craved with her morning coffee.

The day had dawned bright and clear, but there was a storm on the horizon. Strong winds out of the west were pushing the frigid air—fragrant with the sweet smell of fresh water and the spicy scent of pine across Christmas Tree Cove—into Morgan's face as she smiled up at the house at the corner of Hillcrest and Pine.

Built as a summer home for a Chicago shipping magnate at the beginning of the twentieth century, Hillcrest House was a big, white Victorian mansion. The most dramatic feature—Morgan's third-floor tower bedroom—looked as if it was dangerously perched high above the waves of Lake Michigan. Morgan picked up her pace as soon as the house came into view.

Dacey had been the last to arrive, pulling up in front of

the house long after sunset in a mood as dark as her tailored work suit. Her hair was pulled back into a high, swinging pony. Her car had stopped moving, but Dacey was still on a conference call as she dragged her luggage up the front walk.

She was the senior vice president at a tech-focused insurance provider. The last time she'd visited Christmas Tree Cove, she'd been attached to a laptop or constantly buzzing cell phone, speaking a corporate language Morgan didn't understand. Dacey didn't sugarcoat her opinions, even if she begged her to be gentle. Morgan was going to get her honest advice whether or not she asked for it.

"Wow," she said, glancing around the room when her call finally ended. "Nothing has changed."

"What were you expecting?" Morgan asked.

"On the bright side, everything in the kitchen is in the same place Mom kept it," Eli said. "Morgan hasn't rearranged anything."

Morgan smiled. "You'll thank me when we're cooking Thanksgiving dinner tomorrow."

"I've been eating gas station snacks all day. What's for dinner?" Dacey asked.

Morgan laughed. "I've been so busy prepping for Thanksgiving, I forgot."

"Let's order pizza," Eli said.

Within an hour, two large pizzas had been delivered to Hillcrest House. Eli built a fire in the fireplace, and they ate on the sofa in the living room with their stocking feet on the coffee table.

Morgan shoved a huge bite of pizza crust into her mouth and washed it down with a swig from a long-necked bottle of beer. She hadn't been this blissfully happy in so very long. After her parents died, she'd told herself she'd postpone her grief until all the details of the funeral had been arranged. By then, stuffing away the feelings she didn't like had become a habit. It was how she was able to get through another day.

Week. Month. Year.

Morgan didn't have time for emotions. She wasn't even aware she'd been so lonely until after Eli and Dacey arrived.

The creepy knocks of the old, rusty plumbing and the grind of the ancient furnace when it turned in the dark of night were masked by the sounds of Eli's and Dacey's teasing laughter as they yelled insults back and forth from their bedrooms across the hall from each other.

She'd fallen asleep with a smile on her face.

MORGAN RETURNED FROM her errands, slipped quietly into the house through the door in the kitchen and put the grocery bags on the counter. She was surprised to find Dacey sitting at the table enjoying a cup of coffee.

"I didn't think you'd be up for hours."

"I can't sleep in," Dacey said.

Morgan checked her iPhone. "In that case, do you want

to help me get dinner started?"

"Let's do it." Dacey grinned.

By late afternoon the alluring smell of roasted turkey and pumpkin spice wafted out of the kitchen and permeated every inch of Hillcrest House. Eli put himself in charge of making ice and setting the table. By the time Jeff and Kayla arrived, Morgan and Dacey had enough food to feed all of Christmas Tree Cove arranged on the buffet in the dining room.

Everyone's plates were heaped to overflowing as they sat down at the table. No one had time to talk, too busy filling their mouths to speak.

"This is good," Eli said. He raised his glass. "To Adair family traditions."

Everyone clinked their glasses together and took sips of their beverages.

"They still put the buoy out in the harbor," Morgan said.

Dacey and Kayla looked up and smiled.

"Buoy? In the harbor? What are you talking about?" Jeff asked. Kayla's husband was a deputy in the county sheriff's department. He was always on the lookout for anyone who might be stepping outside of the law.

Morgan smiled. "The floating Christmas tree. It was a holiday tradition in Christmas Tree Cove for a very long time. Almost one hundred years."

"A floating Christmas tree in the harbor?" Jeff asked, shaking his head. He hadn't grown up in Christmas Tree

Cove, having moved to the area five years ago. "What are you talking about?"

"Seriously? The tree is gone?" Dacey was apoplectic, her voice laced with rising panic. She discarded her last bite of pie on her plate in disgust.

Kayla shook her head. "No one has put a floating tree on Christmas Tree Cove in many years."

Dacey crossed her arms over her chest. "This is an outrage."

"When we were little," Dacey explained, "a floating Christmas tree would make a mysterious appearance in the harbor on Christmas Eve."

"Whoever did it always timed it perfectly to when the church services were letting out," Kayla agreed.

"Dad said it was Santa's way of letting us know he'd dropped off our Christmas gifts," Eli said.

"Oh, grow up," Dacey said, smacking him on the shoulder.

"Whatever. Believe what you want. When the tree was in the harbor, our presents were under the tree at home," Eli added.

"A little tree covered in fairy lights, riding the waves in a dingy," Dacey remembered.

"It was a dive raft," Kayla insisted. "And a six-foot tree with colored lights."

"It was both," Morgan said. "The tree was different every year. Mom and I stayed up every year to see it, from the tower room, after everyone else had gone to bed."

"It was Mom's favorite holiday tradition," Eli remembered.

Morgan's throat tightened. "Dad said there had never been a year without the tree in over a hundred years. No matter the weather. Then suddenly it was gone."

"But no one knows who did it or why it suddenly disappeared?" Jeff asked.

Morgan shook her head.

"Did you see it the night of the accident?" Dacey wondered.

Morgan nodded. "I caught a glimpse of it from the window in the tower room. Right before you guys came home."

"So let's say whoever was putting the tree out isn't able to do it anymore—shouldn't someone else step up and take over?" Kayla said.

Eli laughed. "I doubt there's a list of people who want to tow a lighted evergreen out into the harbor on a snowy night."

"Christmas Tree Cove still has other holiday traditions," Morgan suggested. "Like caroling in Town Square."

Every year, while the rest of the town was gathered to sing Christmas carols, Morgan and Jesse had met on the bench behind Obermeyer's fishing shanty. The choir director always saved "Silent Night" for the last song of the night. Morgan and Jesse would say good night and find a way to artfully blend into the crowd as they walked back to their cars.

What do you love more? All the twinkling stars scattered across the inky black of a midwinter sky? Or the brightly colored lights reflected across the water from the tree on Christmas Tree Cove?

Morgan smiled, her mind drifting to images of Jesse, past and present.

She was lost in the haze of warm, fuzzy romantic memories until suddenly her daydream was coldly interrupted. It was as if a needle had screeched across a vinyl album of her favorite Christmas songs.

"By the way, I'm not coming home for Christmas. I've been invited to go snowboarding in Lake Tahoe," Eli stated flatly.

"I told my boss if I could get Thanksgiving off," Dacey said, "I'd work over Christmas."

"I've got to work on Christmas too," Jeff said.

"Then we'll probably go to his parents' house for dinner," Kayla added. "You're welcome to join us, Morgan, so you won't be here all alone."

"I'll be fine," she insisted, masking her emotions with a stiff smile. Jeff's family had always been so kind to her, welcoming her with open arms, but she preferred being alone than with someone else's family at Christmas.

"We've got some big news." Kayla's tone included a big dollop of enthusiasm. "We bought the old Sutton place on Main Street. It'll be closer to work for Jeff, and when we have kids, they can walk to school."

"Oh, I love that place," Morgan enthused.

Kayla took a long pause, sharing a look with Dacey and Eli. Morgan could hear the wheels turning in Kayla's mind, evaluating exactly how to word her next sentence.

"The thing is . . . it's going to need some updates," Kayla said, turning to face Morgan directly. "We could really use some extra cash. I spoke with Dacey and Eli, and unless you have any serious objections, Morgan, we'd like to put Hillcrest House on the market."

"Sell the house?" Morgan asked. Words were hard to come by. It was as if she'd been punched in the gut. "You guys all want to sell Hillcrest House?"

Eli nodded. "We need the money. We all do. You do too."

"But I live here," Morgan said. "We don't need to sell the house. You guys need to come home more often."

The silence was deadly. The moments ticked past as Morgan slowly came to understand the truth. Her brothers and sisters didn't want to spend their holidays at Hillcrest House. They didn't want to return to Christmas Tree Cove. Their lives were moving on, taking them to other places.

"But Hillcrest House is kind of a dreary mess," Kayla said.

Morgan nodded. "You're right. The furnace needs to be replaced. I've got a bucket in the attic under a leak in the roof. And I'm almost positive we've got a poltergeist living in the plumbing in Mom and Dad's bathroom. But all those things can be fixed." She wasn't certain if she was defending herself or the house.

"We'll sell it as is," Kayla said.

"As is?" Morgan asked.

She took a shaky breath. It wasn't lost on her that she was the only member of her family putting up a fight to keep Hillcrest House. She was also the only one who still called it home, but she didn't want to stand in the way of what her brother and sisters wanted.

"Let's get it on the market as soon as possible," Eli suggested.

"Before Christmas?" Morgan asked. "Is this a good time?"

The emotions she'd been holding at bay were threatening to leave their safety zone. Morgan's heart was racing but she fought to maintain a thin veneer of calm.

"Okay," she said. "We'll sell the house."

"Sounds like a plan," Kayla agreed.

"If you're sure you're on board," Dacey said. "Eli has already researched Realtors in the area. We've got an appointment to meet with a top real estate broker on Saturday."

"You're sure you're cool with this?" Kayla asked, searching Morgan's face.

"Yes." Morgan nodded her head. She wanted to shake it side to side. She wanted to say no, but in her heart, there was no way to avoid the truth. It was time. It was the right thing to do. Even if the idea of not being able to call Hillcrest House her home made her jittery.

Kayla let out a sigh of relief. Jeff wiped a hand across his forehead, and Eli stretched and rubbed the back of his neck. But Dacey sat still, studying her older sister's face. Morgan nearly melted under her well-meaning sister's scrutiny.

"Excuse me." Morgan pushed herself to a standing position, her chair scraping across the wooden floor. "I need to check on something." She ran up the stairs.

"Morgan," Eli called after her, but she didn't slow her steps. She had to get away before she lost her resolve to be brave in front of her younger brother and sisters. No matter what. She'd always tried to do the right thing by them.

"I'll be right back," Morgan called over her shoulder as she took the stairs two at a time. She didn't want to reveal how attached she was to Hillcrest House. Or how surprised she was they didn't want to celebrate Christmas in Hillcrest House.

Fifteen minutes later, Dacey knocked, then stuck her head into the tower room. "You okay?"

"I'm so sorry," Morgan whispered. Her eyes red-rimmed with emotion. "I can't imagine having Christmas anywhere other than here. When we were kids, it was so magical."

Dacey pressed her index finger to her lips. "Not another word." She sat down next to Morgan on the window seat. Wrapping her arms around her sister's shoulders, Dacey smoothed her hand down Morgan's dark braid.

"I've been so focused on making sure everyone was doing okay that I didn't see this conversation coming. I didn't consider the possibility of selling Hillcrest House," Morgan said. "I thought it would be ours forever. It hit me like a freight train."

"Tell me what you're thinking. Be honest."

Morgan was silent for a moment. "Honestly, it's the right thing to do. To sell the house."

"What will you do?" Dacey asked. "Where will you live?"

Morgan shrugged. "I don't know. It's been so long since I've allowed myself to dream, I'm not sure I can anymore."

"Close your eyes and take the first step."

Morgan took a deep breath. "Easier said than done. Which direction should I go? If I pick the wrong path, will it be too late to start over again? I'm not a kid anymore, and I . . ." She stopped herself before she burdened her sister with her emotions.

Be brave.

Morgan closed her eyes, willing herself not to focus on the hopes and dreams she'd delayed for six years. Everything she'd given up without complaint wasn't within her reach any longer. But she wasn't going to dwell on the negative. Not today. Not while Eli and Dacey were in town.

"You don't talk. You never talk about Mom and Dad. Not one word," Dacey added. Her anxious eyes searched Morgan's face. "Sure you're okay?"

"I'm fine," Morgan lied, a reflexive response to the question she'd been asked too many times. "Correction. I'll be fine.

"Are you sure?" Dacey asked.

"Sometimes I say things out loud that I mean for Mom to hear, then I get frustrated at not being able to hear her voice answer me," Morgan said. "Does that ever happen to you?"

Dacey bit her lip, taking time to choose her words. "I've never done that. Don't get me wrong. I miss them. I do. It's not as painful now as it was back then. I really wish Dad could've walked Kayla down the aisle . . ." She drifted off.

"Eli looked so ridiculous in that tux." Morgan giggled. "It was like three sizes too big."

"And three sizes too short." Dacey shook her head. "He insists he didn't make a mistake, but he must've transposed his inseam and waist measurements. Never would've happened if Mom had been there."

"Almost every day I wish I could talk to them," Morgan said. "To tell them that we're all okay. They'd be so proud of all you guys have accomplished."

"I want to say something bold. You can tell me to hold my tongue, but will you listen instead?"

Morgan nodded.

"I'm not convinced you're living your best life in Christmas Tree Cove," Dacey said. "You're treading water, drowning in a giant fishbowl full of painful memories."

"You've moved on. You're on top of your game," Morgan said. "So you've forgotten—"

"No. *You've* forgotten," Dacey said. "We remember. We *all* remember who you used to be. You were completely fearless. The boldest one of us all."

"I wish . . ." Morgan stopped herself. Anything she said would be a magical reimagining of the past. "I promised myself I would stop starting sentences with phrases like 'I wish' or 'what if' that ended with 'didn't die.'"

"Me too," Dacey assured her. "I've been through it all. I've reasoned, argued, bargained, and made every kind of deal you can imagine with God."

"Maybe it was for the best," Morgan said. "Not that they're gone, but that Mom and Dad went together. They never had to miss each other. At least that's how I comfort myself when you guys aren't here, and I start to miss them too much."

"But we're all here now."

"I'm so grateful we're all together for Thanksgiving," Morgan said.

"Eli and I are going to The Sip. A local brewery is doing a tasting flight. Do you want to join us?" Dacey asked.

Keeping her eyes focused on her fingers so her sister wouldn't see the hurt lurking behind her eyes, Morgan said, "I've got an early flight in the morning."

"You're not staying home alone, are you?"

Morgan shook her head, then got to her feet and put her

hand out to draw her sister up. "I'm going to run over and see Mrs. Kimura," she said. "I'll probably be back before you guys get back from The Sip."

Morgan and Dacey went down the stairs together. Eli walked out of the kitchen, wiping his hands on a towel. "Everything all right?" he asked.

"I'm sorry," Morgan apologized. "I've been living in Hillcrest House for so long. It's the only home I've ever known."

"Not your fault. We dropped a bomb on you." His voice was soft and sympathetic. "We don't have to put the house on the market right now. We can wait until the spring." He glanced at Dacey and reconsidered. "Until you're ready."

Morgan smiled, grateful for her brother's consideration. "No. You're right. It's time. For me. And Hillcrest House. We both need a bit of sprucing up."

"You're sure?" he asked.

"Positive." Morgan hugged her brother. "Did Kayla and Jeff already leave?"

Eli nodded. "They were headed over to his parents for the dessert course, but they stayed long enough to help with the dishes. Which, by the way, did not escape my notice that you both managed to avoid." He crossed his arms over his chest. "If I didn't know better, I'd assume you two had a little after-dinner heart-to-heart in the tower room all planned out in advance."

Morgan shook her head, laughing. "You have the mind

of a villain." She picked up her jacket from the coat tree near the front door. "I'm going over to the Kimuras. Have a good time tonight. Be careful driving back in the snow."

"No worries," Dacey assured her. "We grew up in the Northwoods too."

Crossing the street, Morgan stopped and looked back at Hillcrest House. The big tower house where she'd grown up as a part of one big, loud, confusing family filled with love and laughter was hidden in the shadows by unkempt, snow-covered evergreens. The house was dark and foreboding, with peeling paint and crooked shutters hanging next to the windows.

Hillcrest House looks haunted.

"It is haunted," Morgan whispered. "And I'm the ghost of Christmases past living in it."

Chapter Four

JESSE DREADED GOING over to his mom and dad's house for Thanksgiving dinner. He wasn't in the mood to listen to the latest gossip his mom had collected at the Bait & Tackle Co. during the week. He didn't want to sit in the family room with his dad and fake an interest in professional sports.

He was being aided and abetted by Pops, who strangely wasn't begging to go over to Mom and Dad's house early to watch football.

"I'm going down to Fish Village for a bit," Jesse said. "Do you want to come along?"

Pops jumped to his feet. "What're you going to do down there?"

Jesse shrugged. "Thought I might take some pictures of Sugar Hill from the dock."

"Should've known," Pops said, shaking his head. He was downright giddy about going down to Fish Village. Before Jesse had time to grab his camera bag, Pops was already starting up the truck.

Christmas Tree Cove was unusually quiet on Thanksgiving. A few people were out exercising before sitting down for a big turkey dinner, but the harbor parking lot and Fish Village were both completely deserted.

Jesse and Pops walked down the gravel path together and separated at the docks. Pops headed down to the Taylor fish shanty to do some stuff he'd been putting off. Jesse walked to the end of the river, where there was an unparalleled view of Christmas Tree Cove and the snow-covered pine tree forest on Sugar Hill.

He quickly snapped off a couple of photographs, then stopped. His focus was scattered. Everywhere he looked, all he could see was Morgan. Her smile. Her bewitching eyes.

He'd always marched to the beat of his own drummer, zigging when everyone else was zagging. Morgan was a cheerleader and hung out with the popular girls, but it didn't matter to her that he was different. He'd fallen head over heels for her, and she'd broken his heart. He'd poured himself into his art, determined to become a sought-after freelance commercial photographer. He'd moved to New York City because that's where the work was, but city life wasn't his scene. The more successful he became, the more the only vista he wanted to see through the viewfinder on his camera was within a twenty-five-mile radius of Christmas Tree Cove.

Morgan loved this part of the world as much as he did. There were so many times over the past six years when he wanted to show her a photograph he'd taken. She'd always been his biggest fan and his greatest critic. When she'd turned her back on him, he'd lost more than her love. They'd been each other's guide through the ups and downs of life. Over the years they'd been apart he'd learned to trust himself, but now every time he closed his eyes, there she was smiling up at him.

Jesse shook his head. He wasn't sure how long he'd been standing on the end of the dock when his mom texted, asking if he and Pops had gotten lost and needed directions to their house. He figured he'd avoided his family's Thanksgiving celebration for long enough, so he went back to the fish shanty to gather up Pops and go out to the truck.

By the time they arrived at his parents' house, Dad had finished carving the turkey, and Mom was arranging all the fixings on the buffet in the dining room. Aurora had spent most of the day watching football and was now helping herself to a heaping pile of mashed potatoes with a level of concentration usually reserved for splitting atoms.

"How was your flight yesterday?" Mom asked. Sliding into her seat at the dining room table, she looked innocent, but Jesse wasn't fooled. He glanced at Aurora. She was pouring gravy over everything on her plate. Oh yes. His sister had spilled the beans. He picked up a plate and passed it to Pops. "Same as ever."

"I heard your pilot looked an awful lot like Morgan Adair," Pops said.

"Yep." Jesse nodded.

Pops had never been one to hold his tongue when it came to passing opinions about members of the Adair family. The two rival fishing families had coexisted in Fish Village for several generations, but in the end, the Taylors were the last family standing.

"Skip says Morgan's a mighty fine pilot," Dad said.

Jesse shrugged. "She got us here in one piece, but it's hard for me to judge anyone's skills as a pilot when I'm usually in the back of the plane fighting off motion sickness."

"He was completely green when we splashed down in the harbor yesterday," Aurora giggled, flashing a sympathetic smile in his direction. "I can't believe you and Morgan ever hung out together in high school. She is very cool. And you are very . . ."

"Say it," Jesse challenged his little sister, who valued style over substance.

"Awk-weird."

"Morgan and Jesse were in the same class in school," Dad said. "They started kindergarten together."

"We weren't aware of each other until middle school," Jesse said between mouthfuls. He tried to concentrate on his meal. He had no idea why Pops had dropped Morgan's name into the conversation, but now that it had started, Jesse wanted it to an end as soon as possible. The subject was fraught with danger. If he said one more word about her, he was afraid his family would guess the truth about his feelings for Morgan if they hadn't already.

"She was always a daredevil. Never did anything by half," Mom said. "And with all that gorgeous dark hair trailing behind her wherever she went, she was hard to miss. That's probably why she got into so much trouble. She was such a beautiful girl."

"She still is," Jesse said defensively. Mom was talking about Morgan as if she was an old woman without any future, rather than someone who hadn't even turned thirty yet.

"She was in the grocery store last week. She looked so skittish. She practically faded into the background. She hardly resembled the bold and beautiful girl I used to know," Mom said.

Jesse dropped his silverware on his plate with a clatter. "The woman I was with yesterday was more beautiful that the girl I knew in high school." His words came out sharper than he'd intended. He glanced at Pops, who was making a remarkable effort to stay out of the discussion he'd started by keeping his eyes on his plate.

His mother huffed. No words. Just a sound.

"Morgan used to beat up the boys who made fun of you for being so tall," Dad said, sparing a quick glance in his direction.

Jesse shook his head. Why couldn't they give it a rest?

"And skinny." Mom laughed.

Aurora giggled too. "You were always too skinny."

"Still am," he agreed with a grin.

"I don't understand why she never left Christmas Tree Cove," Mom said. "All the other Adair kids have moved on. Eli's got his own business. Kayla got her teaching degree, and Dacey's a big corporate mucky-muck in Chicago. It's only Morgan who doesn't seem to be going anywhere."

"She's fine," Jesse insisted. "She was very excited Eli and Dacey were home for Thanksgiving."

"Maybe they'll finally do something about that old house," Dad said.

"Like what?" Jesse asked.

"Put it on the market." Mom nodded. "Should've done it years ago."

"Seriously?" Jesse asked. "The Adairs are selling Hillcrest House?" He couldn't imagine Morgan living anywhere other than the tower room high up on the cliff above the harbor.

"Crystal Mayes, that real estate lady from Juniper Point, was in the Bait & Tackle Co. last week, and she mentioned Eli asked her for an appraisal of Hillcrest House," Dad said.

Jesse's stomach dropped. If her brother and sisters wanted to sell the big old house, Morgan would be devastated.

"See, that's the kind of gossip I want you to share," Mom said, shaking her head. "All you ever talk about is how much fish you caught."

"That's important to me," Jesse's dad protested.

"Eli Adair is hot. Is he a nice guy?" Aurora blurted out.

"He's not as nice as me," Jesse said with a smile, relieved the conversation had moved on to an Adair other than

Morgan.

Mom laughed. "Jesse's nice to everybody."

"He's sitting here now, saying how beautiful Morgan is," Aurora said. Jesse's cheeks were flaming with heat. "But as soon as we arrived at the airport, they were circling each other on the tarmac, like they were locked into an octagon for a mixed martial arts world title fight."

"That's not true," Jesse lied.

Mom shook her head. "Not surprised. Morgan Adair was always so fierce."

"She was my best friend," Jesse challenged.

"But you guys never hung out," Mom said. "Ever."

"They were like oil and vinegar before the plane took off," Aurora insisted. "Once we were in flight, Jesse was too busy trying to keep his lunch down to put up much of a fight."

"Which one are you?" Pops asked. "Oil or vinegar?"

"I'm oil," Jesse joked, appreciating the chance to lighten the tone of the conversation. "Morgan is an elderflower-infused white vinegar."

"Oil and vinegar?" Mom asked. "That makes vinaigrette. Which, as you know, is lovely and delicious."

"Yep. Morgan and I are a vinaigrette," Jesse agreed.

His mom ignored him. "What I think you mean is, Jesse and Morgan are like oil and water, Aurora."

"What I mean is, you guys don't get along. At all," Aurora said.

"We get along fine," Jesse said, pressing his lips together to keep from revealing he and Morgan had never been enemies.

Mom shook her head. "I just don't understand. What ever happened to her?"

"Her parents died," Jesse said. His tone was harsh. He wished again that Morgan Adair wasn't the topic of discussion at his family's Thanksgiving dinner.

"I know that, Jesse. It was terrible. I went to the funeral," she said.

"She won't step foot in Fish Village," Pops added.

The conversation continued on, but Jesse drifted off again.

His memories of Fish Village were all about Morgan. The time they spent together behind Obermeyer's ramshackle shack on a wooden bench with an incredible view of the beach and Lake Michigan beyond. A spot hidden away from the rest of the world. Where Morgan and Jesse could dream about their future.

They'd kept each other's secrets. All this time.

Did she ever think about him? Probably not. And maybe that was for the best.

Chapter Five

THE KIMURAS LIVED in a snug and cozy Christmas cottage on the steep incline directly across Pine Street from Hillcrest House. An award-winning gardener, Mrs. Kimura had been trained in the art of ikebana and had worked alongside her husband at the Forget-Me-Not Flower Shop for thirty years.

Some of Morgan's first memories were following Mrs. Kimura around in her garden on her daily planting chores. Mrs. Kimura had been her unofficial babysitter, but to Morgan, she was her own fairy godmother.

Even in the middle of winter, Mrs. Kimura's cottage garden was alive and flourishing, filled with spicy winter scents: pine, rosemary, and a hint of winterberries. Birds fluttered in the branches of the trees, and little woodland creatures had left paw prints in the fresh snow.

Morgan admired the flower boxes under the windows of the little Cape Cod, overflowing with pine boughs, holly berries, and twinkling white fairy lights. She stomped the snow off her shoes on the front porch before she knocked.

"Morgan?" Mrs. Kimura opened the front door. "I

thought you'd be with your brother and sisters tonight."

"Me too," Morgan said, forcing a grin. "But then Dacey and Jeff left for his parents' house. And Kayla and Eli went off to The Sip. I have to get up early in the morning to do a run up to Torch Lake. So I stopped by to see how you're doing."

Morgan drew the petite woman, dressed in khakis and a Patagonia jacket, in for an embrace. Her hair was glossed with bits of silver, but when she smiled, she glowed with energy.

Whenever Morgan was feeling blue, a visit with the Kimuras always cheered her up.

"You're in luck," Mrs. Kimura said warmly.

"Guess who made gingerbread this morning?" Mr. Kimura said with a wink.

Mrs. Kimura's gingerbread was famous in Christmas Tree Cove. She served it warm from the oven with a vanilla crème anglaise. Morgan craved the taste during the holidays.

"I guess it's a good thing I showed up when I did," she said.

Morgan followed Mr. Kimura into the living room. The decorating inside the small house was crisp and tasteful, as was almost everything Mrs. Kimura did. Morgan sat down in a chair near the fire. Mr. Kimura sat down in his spot on the sofa.

"How was your Thanksgiving?" he asked.

She smiled. "I didn't burn the turkey. So I'm calling that

a win. It's nice to have other people in the house. I wasn't aware of how lonely I'd been, living alone all this time."

Mrs. Kimura carried a tray full of treats in from the kitchen. "Here we are. So, tell us, how is everybody doing?" she asked while her husband served the treats. "What's the news from your brother and sisters?"

"Eli's brewery in Ann Arbor is doing great," Morgan explained. "And Dacey will soon own Chicago if she doesn't already. What about you guys?" Morgan changed the topic, digging into the gingerbread. "How was your Thanksgiving?"

"Quiet," Mr. Kimura said. "Which is what we wanted. Especially since—"

"We're not keeping the flower shop open after the holidays," Mrs. Kimura cut him off. "We'll be here for Christmas, then we'll leave right after. We'll reopen again in April for spring planting season."

Morgan's heart was being squeezed as if in a vise, but she forced herself to hold a tight smile on her face. The Kimuras were her favorite people on earth. They didn't know she wouldn't get through the winter without her paycheck from the flower shop.

Morgan took a big bite of gingerbread. "Oh. This is delicious."

Mrs. Kimura smiled. She loved compliments. "How long will Eli and Dacey stay?"

"Through the weekend. But they won't be here for

Christmas."

Mr. and Mrs. Kimura exchanged a glance. "That's becoming a tradition, isn't it? Not coming home for Christmas."

"Well, I'll go with Jeff and Kayla to his parents' house. I won't be alone," Morgan said. She was lying. She'd rather be alone on Christmas than celebrate with people she didn't love.

"You can spend Christmas with us," Mrs. Kimura said, looking delighted.

Morgan nodded. But she had a hard time working up any enthusiasm for Christmas, even while Mr. Kimura was reminiscing about Christmases past. Usually she loved his stories, but not tonight. Morgan sat quietly, waiting for her first chance to escape.

Glancing at her iPhone, she remarked, "I've got an early flight, and I really should be going."

The Kimuras both nodded and walked her to the door.

"Stop by next week," Mrs. Kimura said, waving goodbye. "I'll need your help with the Christmas terrariums."

"Will do." Morgan said, willing her voice to sound cheerful. "Thank you again for the gingerbread."

She was out the door and walking down the sidewalk before she'd had the chance to process the Kimuras' announcement about their plans to keep the store closed all winter. She'd forgot to tell them about putting Hillcrest House up for sale.

It didn't matter. She wasn't sure she was ready to tell them. As soon as Mrs. Kimura heard the news, the reaction on her face would make Morgan's changing circumstances too real for her to handle.

STRONG WINDS BLOWING up the cliff from the lake nearly knocked her over as she crossed the street to Hillcrest House. She stopped in the middle of the street, and suddenly an impossibly perfect glimpse of Lake Michigan in all its glory came into view. The stars were so bright in the winter sky she could almost reach out and touch them.

Her mother had always covered the trees around Hill-crest House with fairy lights at Christmas, but tonight the overgrown evergreens created a dark fortress around the house.

"Hillcrest House needs to be merry," she said out loud to herself.

Navigating snow drifts in the driveway, she went to the garage where she found some colored fairy lights and pine roping. She carried the mess of electrical wires and fake evergreen to the front porch. On tiptoes, she made quick work of hanging the decorations above the front door, but within minutes her fingers had lost all their dexterity in the frigid night air.

Gloves. Gloves would be good here.

"Hey," someone whispered from the dark evergreens behind her.

Morgan screamed loud and long, tumbling off the porch into the snow-covered shrubbery. Her tonsils burned like they'd been scraped by a surgical tool. She was surprised to find herself face-to-face with Jesse for the second time in as many days. He was laughing as he extended a hand to help her up.

"Jesse Taylor. Of course, it's you," she said. She was stuck, but still hesitated before taking his hand and letting him pull her out of the bushes and back on her feet. "What are you doing up here?" she asked.

He held up his Leica. "I came by to take some photos."

"But you live on the other side of town," she challenged.

"You've got the best view of the harbor at night." Jesse pointed to a spot directly beneath her tower bedroom. "And photos of Christmas Tree Cove are the bread and butter of my website."

She made a face. "It's been my view for twenty-nine years."

"*Your* view?" He shook his head. "Damn. The Adairs are always so possessive."

"Seriously? Everything my family has ever owned has been bought by the Taylors."

Jesse was in the shadows, but she heard him make a low, guttural sound. She'd finally managed a direct hit to his ego. "What are you doing out here?"

She gestured toward the pine bunting and Christmas lights she'd attempted to hang over the door. "Putting up a little Christmas."

"It's after ten o'clock," he protested.

"But I really needed some Christmas cheer."

Jesse smiled. He was devastatingly beautiful. The dark stubble of his beard along his chin. His curls perfectly tousled in the chill wind. And his eyes icy blue in the silvery moonlight.

When Jesse looked at her without animosity, her troubles faded away. When it was just the two of them . . . Jesse and Morgan.

Their relationship had always played out like this. During the day, they'd snapped and snarled like cats fighting over the catch of the day on the docks. As soon as the sun went down, they'd found their way into each other's arms. Something happened under the light of the night sky.

Jesse stood back and looked at the decorations Morgan had hung up over the front door. He tilted his head from side to side like a confused puppy. "I'm not sure your decoration qualifies as 'cheer.'"

"What's wrong with it?" She took a step back. She didn't need Jesse's confirmation to recognize it as the ugliest, most ill-conceived Christmas decoration anyone had ever put up.

"It's leaning to one side," he said, holding up his hand at a thirty-degree angle for emphasis.

Morgan blew out her frustration. "I've been trying to fix

it, but my fingers are numb. I've lost all my dexterity." She opened and closed her hands, her knuckles stiff with cold, her frustration quickly getting the best of her.

"Where are your gloves?" he asked.

She shook her head. "I'm not sure. I left the house in a hurry."

He made an animal sound deep in his throat that made her turn and look at him. Then he took her right hand in his large gloved one and pushed it into the right-front pocket of his vest. He did the same with her left hand.

Her nose was pressed into the warmth of his quilted vest. She looked up to see his face and nearly swooned. When did she forget how handsome he was?

She closed her eyes. They'd been friends for so long. Her memory wasn't good enough to recall the first time a glance from him made her heart skip a beat, but right now she was only too aware she was still under his spell.

He took a step closer to the front door. She took a step back. It was as if they were rehearsing for some strange push-me pull-you race at a Fourth of July picnic. She closed her eyes and pushed her hands deeper into the pockets of his down vest. Her hands unfurled and embraced the warmth. Her fingers brushed over a hard candy wrapped in cellophane in one pocket.

"You can have the peppermint," he said.

She glanced up at his bearded chin. Knowing he was the kind of man who carried hard candy in his pockets did nothing to diminish her attraction to him.

"So, what happened?"

"What?"

"You had a bad day. Tell me about it."

She shook her head. "No. No thanks. I'm good."

"You don't look like it was good," he said.

"Thanks."

"What I mean is, I'm right here. And you're alone. And since we don't run in the same circles anymore, I'm safe. You can tell me about your feelings," he coaxed. "I'm like a disinterested third party. So, tell me, Morgan. How was your day?

Morgan licked her lips, pausing for a moment to consider his offer.

She hadn't been this close to Jesse in years, and yet she trusted him. It was both comforting and disquieting. And she liked the idea of being able to speak freely with someone without having to worry about her emotions. "I checked the forecast, and we're due for a deep freeze next week. That means the harbor will freeze over and I won't be flying for the next four months after that," she said. "Which is not unexpected—it happens every year. But the Kimuras are keeping the flower shop closed through March."

"Shit," Jesse swore.

Morgan nodded. "And I live pretty close to the bone."

"So things will be tight without a paycheck to cover you through the winter months until you're airborne again," he said.

"Yep. And my brother and sisters want to sell the house," she whispered, dropping the bomb sotto voce.

"Ouch," he said. "That's gotta sting."

She nodded silently. Jesse didn't say another word, letting a comfortable silence hang in the air between them. It was almost as if he was waiting for her to get control over her emotions again before he asked more questions. "Do you have any plans?"

Be brave.

She'd been telling herself that for the past six years, but maybe it was time to be honest. "No. I was completely blindsided by the idea. But I don't want to stand in their way."

"Are you okay?" His voice was gentle, his lips so close. Just feeling his breath on the shell of her ear sent tingles of pleasure down her spine.

"What? Yes. Of course. I'm fine," Morgan responded a bit too quickly. "I'm perfectly fine."

"You're always fine." He fixed her with a glare and she nearly hyperventilated.

Jesse's eyes were so blue. His dimples so deep. He looked like a really angry movie star.

She needed to take a step away from him. They were too close. Normal people in this position would hug. Or kiss. Their lips were inches apart. If Jesse bent down and she stood on her tippy toes, it was totally possible.

No. She would not be kissing Jesse again. Not in this lifetime.

Definitely not. Kissing Jesse was not an option.

Or was it?

Chapter Six

*D*AMN HER EYES.

Despite everything that had happened between them, as soon as he looked into her eyes, he was bewitched. His heart had never belonged to anyone other than Morgan. And he still cared about her. More than he wanted to admit.

Matt Wendell had emailed him a few more details about the job. Matt was right. The job was perfect for him. Working full time in New York City would help him move on.

But was that really what he wanted?

Whenever he was back in Fish Village, he'd find himself looking up at Hillcrest House on the cliff high above, wondering if Morgan was all right. He'd stayed away from her. Never coming too close. The few times he'd glimpsed her from across the street or around the corner, she'd looked guarded, so he'd kept his distance. He could ignore his broken heart, but he wasn't always in control of his emotions around her.

Maybe he should not have acquiesced when she'd asked for time and space after her parents died. Maybe she didn't really want to be alone. He'd always taken everyone and everything at face value. Had she been telling the truth?

What if she'd been lying? It had been so easy for her to take a step back from their relationship without an explanation. Emotionless. Cold-blooded and cruel.

He glanced at her face. She'd taken a few steps away from him now, standing silently and studying him in the dark. It was unnerving.

She was clenching her fists. No doubt her fingers were cold, and there was no way she was going to put her hands in his vest again.

"Here," he said. "Take my gloves."

He shoved the old leather gloves in her direction. She put them on immediately while he struggled with some words of comfort.

"Change is hard," he stated matter-of-factly.

She nodded, but in the darkness, he wasn't able to discern any reaction on her face. "I don't want to discuss anything too personal."

He nodded. "Absolutely not. I don't either. As a disinterested third party, my advice is maybe you should approach your brother's and sisters' desire to sell the house as a strictly business decision. They've said what they want. Now, you negotiate your terms."

"What kind of terms?"

"Look. I work freelance. When I'm negotiating with an advertising agency for a photo shoot, they tell me what they want. Then I tell them what they need to give me in order to make that happen. All business. No emotion," he said. "Your siblings want to sell the house. What do you want?"

"One last family Christmas together," she answered without any prompting.

"Okay. Those are your terms. See how easy it was? No emotions necessary."

She sighed in relief. "That's how I want to live. Emotion-free."

"Sounds about right," he said. She smiled, unaware of his unintentional irony.

Now let's talk about how you shattered my heart into pieces, shall we?

She moved to close the gap between them, if only for body heat. "You smell nice."

"Two-for-one sale on body wash and shampoo at the mercantile." He kept his tone light, hoping she'd give him a bit of physical space. Instead, she moved closer, inspecting his down vest and cashmere sweater as if she were a professional tailor.

"Morgan," he barked, invoking her name like a warning shot. He should take a step back. He should brush her off. He should run like the wind as far away from her as possible. But he was all in.

She pulled back a little. Enough so she could slip the unwrapped peppermint candy from his pocket between her soft, open lips—an act that almost caused him to lose his composure. Hopefully, his skittering heartbeat didn't betray him through his layers of wool-and-down clothing.

Morgan was quiet for a bit, staring off into the darkness over his shoulder.

He refocused his energy on rearranging the Christmas lights over the door, hoping to turn the pine rope and light string into something that looked less like a paramecium through the lens of a microscope. His fingers worked feverishly, separating and disentangling the strands.

He was surprised Morgan was so content not to boss him. She was always in charge, always organizing an activity or event, and always had something to say.

He'd never been able to resist the constant push and pull of conflicting ideas that always existed between them. He was certain their contentious connection was an allure for her too.

I need to pique her ire.

His mind was spinning. She'd always been a fighter. What could he say to get her to engage? With every passing minute, he became more certain the anger she carried so close to the surface was his best bet to connect with her again.

Her nearness was a distraction. He swallowed hard and stared at her mouth for much longer than he should've.

She smiled and leaned closer to him. He didn't pull away or resist when she sniffed the intimate space between his neck and collarbone. A peppermint-scented puff of air from her breath sent tingles of electricity up his spine, making the hair on the back of his neck stand up.

"Stop it," he protested. He was clinging to his self-control by his fingernails. "Stop sniffing me. I'm not an aromatherapy candle."

He took a step back from her and walked down the front steps all the way to the sidewalk, where a frigid blast of lake air helped him gain control over his physical response to her. He gestured with one finger for her to come and stand next to him on the sidewalk in front of the house. "Tell me what you think."

Morgan joined him on the sidewalk with her arms crossed over her chest. Her critical eyes missed nothing as she evaluated the adjustments he'd made to the Christmas display over the front door.

"It's perfect," she said. Her wide-open smile nearly knocked him to his knees. He told himself not to react. He needed to be as controlled with his emotions as she was with hers.

"I should go," he said. "It's late."

She put a hand on his arm and he nearly lost his resolve. "Thanks for your help."

He'd reached the street before he stopped and turned around. "When was the last time you were in Fish Village?"

She shrugged. "Probably the memorial service for my parents."

"It's been that long?" he asked, keeping his voice free of emotion.

She nodded. "I'm not certain I can face all the memories in Fish Village. I'm not strong enough."

"Why don't you come by tomorrow?" He shrugged. "You can lean on me if you need to. As a disinterested third party. I'll buy you a croissant and an Americano. Give you a tour of what's new."

"No. Thanks. Nothing ever changes in Fish Village. That's part of its charm." She laughed.

His heart was beating as if it were trying to get out of his chest. Her green eyes sparkled in the moonlight. "Come by and I'll show you what's new," he suggested again.

She shrugged. "I'm flying a group up to Whitefish Falls first thing in the morning. And then I've got to pick up someone's mother-in-law from Fox Island and return her to Traverse City so she can catch a connecting flight to North Carolina."

Jesse considered her dilemma for a moment. "So instead of an Americano, I'll buy you lunch."

"Maybe." Her answer was quiet, non-committal, and devoid of emotion.

"Liar." He spat out the word, holding his fingers crossed behind his back. "You have no intention of ever returning to Fish Village."

"I am not a liar," she protested, taking the bait he'd dangled right in front of her. "I'll be there. Tomorrow."

He almost cheered when the spark of anger appeared in her eyes. He'd forced her hand, but he had to stay calm and keep lying. "Yeah, right. You're a quitter. You've always been a quitter," he said.

"I am not a liar. Or a quitter," she protested. "Speak for yourself."

Walk away. Walk away now.

He took a step back, shielding his face from her view. He didn't want her to see his smirk. He jammed his hands deep into his pockets and half-walked, half-galloped down the sloping street.

"I'll be there," she shouted after him.

Her angry tone made him grin. Why had it taken him six years to remember she'd never step down from a fight? At least it wasn't too late.

"We'll see," he scoffed.

"What about your gloves?" she shouted, taking a step into the street. She sounded furious. Was she following him?

He hesitated, wanting to go back and smooth her ruffled feathers, but he didn't dare. He kept moving forward, walking away from her as fast as he could after setting the trap and luring the one thing he wanted the most in the world toward it.

His old suede gloves smelled of fish and kerosene. He didn't care if she ever returned them. He liked the idea of her having something of his almost as much as he liked her owing him a favor.

"Keep them," he shouted over his shoulder.

"I'll give them back to you tomorrow," she shouted. He

couldn't see her face, but her voice was laced with attitude. "You better bring your wallet, Jesse Taylor. You're buying lunch. And I'll be hungry."

He snorted under his breath to hide the fact that his heart was about to explode with joy. Morgan was threatening him with what he wanted more than anything else in the world. Spending time with him.

Oh yes. He was totally playing her.

He had to do it her way, and he had to do it right. This time he was playing for keeps.

Chapter Seven

MORGAN STOOD ON the gravel path, looking across the harbor toward Fish Village. Lake Michigan was covered in white-capped waves, and a thick pine forest stretched up to the top of Sugar Hill as far as her eyes could see.

She'd boldly announced she'd have lunch with Jesse. He'd made her angry, on purpose, to get her to come back to Fish Village. At the time, she was up for the challenge. But after he'd left her alone in the darkness in front of Hillcrest House, she'd tossed and turned all night.

When she'd finally closed her eyes, Jesse was standing on the deck of the fishing tug, looking back over the water, a storm rolling in over the growing waves on Lake Michigan.

Sweet. Kind. Hunky.

She hadn't walked away from Jesse. She'd run. As fast as possible. And she'd never looked back because it had been easier to focus on what needed to get done after her parents died.

Maybe it was unkind.

It was all her fault. She should've talked to Jesse. She

should've answered his calls.

Her cheeks bloomed with heat. She'd been very flirty last night.

Now under a bright-blue sky on a clear winter day, she wasn't certain she could face him. She was suddenly aware of emotions she hadn't allowed herself to have in so long. Emotions like hope and desire. Both probably written in indelible ink on her face every time she glanced at Jesse.

She walked to the end of the path and stopped before stepping out onto the docks. She blew out an anxious breath and took her first step.

Be brave.

The planks crisscrossing the weatherworn dock had been upgraded in the fifties to replace the docks that the original settlers had built at the turn of the twentieth century. Morgan focused on the uneven surface. When she was younger, she'd memorized the size and shape of each plank along this section of dock. She and her dad had given them nicknames. Greeting each board beneath her feet, she stepped on Carona, "the one with the rounded end." She smiled at the one with a hint of bark from the tree from which it was hewn—she and Dad had named it Spot. She stepped over Knute, the "one with the knothole" you could see the water through. Each one was a connection to her past.

At first glance, nothing in Fish Village had changed. Her eyes grew misty. All the familiar fishing shanties, smokehouses, and drying racks were still there. Farther down the docks, two familiar fish tugs, *Faith* and *Dorthea Lou*, were tied off on each side of the docks overhanging the water.

She stopped in front of the now-deserted shanties that had once housed her family's fishing business. It seemed like only yesterday when Dad used to be out on the boat and Mom behind the counter of the Bait & Tackle Co. gourmet foods and spices. Young Morgan had no idea those days would be so fleeting.

Cupping her hands on the icy windowpane, Morgan peered inside the gourmet grocery store. She recognized the bags of roasted pistachios and English toffee in colorful Christmas tins stacked almost all the way to the ceiling. She pushed through the door with a smile on her face and was almost knocked to the ground by the savory mix of scents in the store.

Herby hints of dill and the sharp tang of mustard and oregano hung in the air. A few shoppers mingled in the pasta and tomato sauce aisle, but the biggest crowd by far had gathered near the deli, where a take-a-number machine kept fights from breaking out between the people waiting for the award-winning sandwiches that were prepared for daily sack lunches.

She hadn't had breakfast, and her stomach rumbled in protest. A high school girl in a white apron wiped her hands on a towel and smiled as Morgan approached the counter.

"Can I help you?" she asked.

"Is Jesse around?"

She smiled brightly. "He was here earlier. I think he's out with Dot."

"She is his first love," Morgan said, shaking her head.

"She's his one true love."

Morgan spun around.

Mrs. Taylor. Petite. Fierce. Glamourous. She was always perfectly styled, her nails manicured in a neutral color. "Well, well, well. If it isn't vinegar looking for oil."

"I beg your pardon?"

"We were talking about you and Jesse at dinner last night," she said.

"We? Who's we? Me? And Jesse?" Morgan stuttered. "There's no such thing."

Jesse's mom smiled knowingly. She shook her head. "You and Jesse. Vinaigrette. Always drawn to each other even though you guys don't get along."

"We. No. We . . . don't do that," Morgan blustered. This was exactly the kind of interaction she'd been hoping to avoid.

Jesse's mom shook her head. "You two. Such a pair."

Morgan put on her best fake smile. "Good to see you again. The place looks great."

She backed up the aisle, hoping she wouldn't trip over someone; then once she was out of sight of Jesse's mom, she ran for the door. Back outside, she tucked her shoulder into the wind and scurried down the docks. She stopped near the moorings where the fishing tugs were tied up.

Dot was Jesse's nickname for the *Dorthea Lou*. The steel-bottomed fishing tug had been in the Taylor family since she was built in the late sixties. Named after Jesse's grandma, she was the same kind of tug as *Faith*, the tug that was moored on the other side of the docks, that was named after her mom.

Jesse was in the aft of the tug, tinkering with the engine. Every fisherman she'd ever known worked on their boat's engine in their free time. No one wanted to break down in the middle of Lake Michigan, especially not on a cold morning in the middle of winter, so maintenance was a daily grind. A rescue on the lake this time of year would be particularly risky.

Morgan swung herself up onto the deck of the boat.

"Stop talking about me behind my back," she said with a blast of sass.

"I haven't said one word about you to anyone," Jesse protested. He never looked up from whatever he was working on. Didn't spare a single glance in her direction.

"Vinaigrette," she said through gritted teeth.

All the color drained from his face. He looked her square in the eye.

"Okay. That was my sister. Not me."

"Is gossiping about the Adairs some weird form of entertainment for you and your family?" Morgan asked.

"You are not and were never . . . entertainment," he protested. "Where did you get that idea?"

The spark in his eyes made her cheeks scald. From anger. Or maybe desire. She wasn't sure. The more she was around Jesse, the more she was starting to have a hard time telling her emotions apart.

Chapter Eight

H<small>E TURNED AWAY</small> and took a moment to catch his breath.

Morgan was standing in the cold, frowning at him. She had an enormous scarf wound around her neck and shoulders. Pink. She loved pink. How could he ever forget her love of color? She'd spent one entire summer in a pink Bugs Bunny sweatshirt and cut-off shorts, wearing it like it was a uniform.

Her scarf was the same color as her cheeks and her lips. He stared at her open mouth, surprised by how much he wanted to kiss her right now.

He needed to find a distraction. And fast.

He crawled out of the hold and replaced the cover. He wiped his hands on a cloth, his eyes on Morgan, studying her with a curious intensity. He put his glasses back on his nose and pushed his long, dark curls out of his eyes in one swipe.

"Where are the gloves I gave you?" he asked.

She pulled them out from her pockets and tossed them on top of the hold. "You can have them back."

"Put them on," he snarled. "It's cold. And you're always

cold."

For once, she didn't argue. His brown work gloves reeked of fish guts and leather, but they gave her an impish Minnie Mouse appeal that made him smile despite his thorny mood.

A cold breeze bounced across the waves of the lake and sliced right through his Carhartt jacket, making the muscles in his back and neck cold and tight. It was a good reminder that he needed to keep his cool where she was concerned.

He jumped off the boat in one easy motion. Before Morgan had the chance to do the same, Jesse reached for her and lifted her up and off the boat. She braced her hands on his shoulders as he set her down on the dock next to him. Her body brushed against his, and Jesse was nearly knocked to his knees. Of one thing he was very certain: six years had passed, but his attraction to Morgan was as potent and heady as ever.

Jesse led Morgan down the docks to Bait & Tackle Co. and held open the door for her.

"Is this what you want to show me?" There was a critical tone to her voice. Her eyes were bright, but her stance was wary. She folded her arms over her body. "Because I already know this place pretty well. In fact, I memorized the menu in high school."

"I promised you lunch," he laughed. "We can get something to go." He went behind the counter and tied an apron around his waist. He grinned. "What'll you have?"

She leaned against a glass display filled with deli meats

and cheeses and looked up at the menu of prepared sandwiches. He waited while she made her decision. He studied her face as she weighed each option, as if she were selecting the menu for a royal banquet. She bit down hard on her lower lip, and he laughed under his breath, earning an annoyed glare from her.

"A pastrami sandwich with olives and cornichons on the side," she said, finally making up her mind.

Jesse went into action behind the counter, slicing bread and filling it with meat. He made a second sandwich for himself, wrapped them both in wax paper and put them in a paper bag with a couple of bags of chips.

He braced himself before he walked back out into the cold, holding the door open for Morgan. Back out on the docks, he led her farther into Fish Village. Away from the harbor. Away from the water. Where the oldest shanties in Fish Village still stood.

"Are we having a picnic?" She smiled softly, and his heart skipped a beat.

"Yep. Follow me," he said with a gesture of his head. "Making a living in Christmas Tree Cove has changed a lot over the past few years. Every year more of the business in Fish Village leans on the tourist industry."

"I'd heard they've issued fewer fishing licenses," Morgan agreed.

Jesse nodded. "There were several years in a row where Lake Michigan was overfished. The DNR stopped issuing licenses for certain fish. I don't think it will ever be the same. Our license for whitefish this year is only 80,000 pounds. Our tug is only going out six, maybe six-and-a-half, months a year."

"What about Pops? Does he still fish?"

Jesse shook his head. "Not for real. In the summer, he'll take a day out. But I usually go, and I have to hire help, which is expensive. I need someone who knows what they're doing."

"Dad always said you couldn't love fishing," Morgan agreed. "You have to be completely devoted to it."

"He was right," he said. "We expanded the smokehouse business too. We not only sell our signature smoked fish, but now we smoke meats and ship them across the country through an online business. Sales of whole smoked turkey has been a lifesaver for us in the winter."

Jesse pointed up ahead, pushing Morgan along the docks with a hand behind her elbow. "Up here, around the corner. I want to show you something."

"The only thing up around the corner is Obermeyer's rickety old shanty."

"Be careful how you talk about her," Jesse said with a playful smile. "She's mine now."

"You bought Obermeyer's?" Morgan stopped walking. "Are you crazy? It's a wreck. It was always teetering on the verge of collapse."

Morgan was right. Obermeyer's shanty was the oldest of

the little wooden shacks that made up Fish Village. The roof pitch was as swayback as an old nag, and the siding was missing more cedar shake shingles than it had nailed to the walls.

Jesse grinned. He was excited to show her all the alterations he'd been working on. The ramshackle little shanty had always had a special place in his heart.

It was their place. His and Morgan's.

Morgan walked around the corner and stopped, staring up at the now beautiful, two-story, cedar shake building with large, plate-glass storefront windows in the spot where Obermeyer's fish shack had been for over a hundred years.

"It's gorgeous. But what about the bench?" she asked.

"It's still there," he said quietly, unable to maintain eye contact with her for fear he'd give away how much it meant to him that her first question was about the bench—their bench. It was the last place they'd ever been together as more than friends. A place his heart hoped they'd be together again. "Still the best view of the harbor."

Her smile reached her eyes.

Jesse opened the door and led her into the large space. The walls of the main room were covered in wood plank paneling.

"We jacked and leveled the old building. Replaced every beam holding up the roof," he said. "Built it new with post and beam to create this soaring two-story space. And then we added some skylights. Because, speaking as a photographer, lighting always matters."

Morgan stood in the middle of the room, spinning in a circle to take in everything about the room. Jesse was still awed by the transformation, even though he'd been a part of it every step of the way.

"This would make HGTV's interior decorators' shiplap-crazy dreams come true." Morgan laughed.

"On the other side, there will be room for an apartment on the second floor."

"You're living in Fish Village?"

He grinned. "Not yet. When I'm in town, I stay with Pops. But now that the first floor is finished, they'll start work on the upstairs apartment in January."

"What do you plan to do with all this amazing space?" she asked, spinning in the center of the room.

"My dream is to be able to afford to live off my income selling fine art photographs. Working as a freelance photographer is a drag. Last summer I had to shoot a couple of weddings."

"Weddings? You? You hate weddings," she teased.

"I don't hate weddings," he corrected. "But I don't like being bossed around, and weddings are ripe for that kind of drama."

She covered her face and laughed. The sound was contagious.

"What?" He feigned innocence.

She tried to regain her composure, but her giggles got the

best of her. "If I had a dime for every time you said, 'You're not the boss of me,' I wouldn't need to a second job over the winter months."

A smile stretched across his face. A warm feeling bubbled up inside of him. It was so good to be with her like this, just having a conversation. It had been too long.

"I want to set up a fine arts photography gallery, but I need help. I'm wearing too many hats. Once Mom and Dad snowbird off to Florida for the winter, I'll have to oversee daily operations at the Bait & Tackle Co. at the same time that I'm bidding and working on freelance assignments in New York, and flying here often enough to keep Pops out of trouble."

"You've got a lot on your plate."

"Too much," he agreed. "That's where you come in."

"Me?" She looked shocked.

"I need someone to set up this gallery. Hang the photographs on the walls. Price them. Set up a system for ordering, in person and online. Work with the electricians on the lighting grid, hire someone to mind the store, and be here when I can't. You organized the Bait & Tackle Co. before it opened. And you've been doing the same kind of thing for the Kimuras at the Forget-Me-Not Flower Shop. Would you be interested in working here? For me?"

She looked up into the post-and-beam rafters soaring above their heads, and then turned and looked him in the eyes. "Why me?"

"I need help," he said, hoping she wouldn't catch on to his lies and half-truths before she agreed. "And you need a paycheck for the winter season."

She nodded enthusiastically. "I do need a job, and it's definitely a good opportunity."

She had always been a chameleon. One minute focused on herself and her own problems, she could flip a switch and her passionate emotions would be available for a loved one to access.

Empathetic. Kind. Loving. Ready to do battle. She had always been invincible.

"But I have one question before we go further. Do we have any unfinished business to discuss?" she asked. Her tone flat and direct. "We left a lot of things unsaid. But now so much time has gone by, I want to make sure we don't have any lingering issues that would make this awkward for either of us before I say 'yes.'"

"No." He took a deep breath before delivering the big lie. "We can both agree that six years ago, we were young and we were in love. And now we're not. That's it for me. What about you?" His heart was beating like a tom-tom drum. He baited his hook, hoping to draw her in. "Do you have any feelings you'd like to discuss?"

"No." She shook her head. Her beautiful face betrayed no emotion. "I've got nothing. I've moved on."

"Me too. I've moved on."

He had no clue he was such a good liar. Maybe that was

why his words tumbled too quickly out of his mouth. He focused on keeping a pleasant smile plastered on his face. At least he hoped it looked like a smile. It was actually more of a wince. Hearing she was completely over him, even after all this time, broke his heart. Again.

They sat down in the middle of the new wooden floor to enjoy a picnic lunch.

"As a bonus, if you're working here, my mother will stay out of my business. She's scared of you."

Morgan snorted, almost shooting pastrami and rye out of her nose. A smile of defiance playing on her face. "Me? I beg your pardon."

"And I trust you," he added, sounding awkward. Not for the first time in his life, his words failed him. This wasn't going as neatly as he'd planned. The sun-filled room was warm, and he was woozy and light-headed. Had he always been like this when he was around her?

"Really?" she asked. "You trust me?"

He leaned forward, searching her face, hoping for a momentary glimpse of any remaining feelings she might have for him. But she turned away. She was still a closed book.

They sat in silence, cross-legged on the floor, with the paper wrappings from the sandwiches and an empty potato chip bag scattered on the wooden floor keeping them apart. The air between them was charged. Morgan avoided any eye contact.

Jesse swallowed hard. He should say something. Anything. Before the connection between them slipped away. He cleared his throat. The door burst opened, ushering in Grace on a cold blast of air.

Jesse jumped to his feet, leaving Morgan scrambling to her feet on her own. "Grace! You remember Morgan, don't you?"

"Our pilot," Grace said. Her sparkling brown eyes smiled at Jesse. She turned to Morgan and gave her a five-second, head-to-toe style assessment. Grace was clearly not impressed. To her credit, Morgan didn't seem to care. Jesse was surprised. When Morgan was younger, she never would've let a flagrant vibe check like that slide. "I'm sorry," Grace said. "Was I interrupting something?"

"Nothing at all," Morgan said. "I was just leaving." She walked across the room to the chair where they'd left their coats and pulled her jacket from the pile. She put it on and wrapped her giant pink scarf around her neck.

"Thanks for lunch." She looked at him with a gleam in her eye that made him wary and anxious. Was she being naughty or nice? "It was delicious. Was that a vinaigrette on the pastrami?"

His eyes narrowed. "No. It was a spicy mustard." His heart skipped a beat.

Naughty. The firecracker he'd fallen for was still there, hidden underneath a giant scarf and a pair of Carhartt overalls.

"Oh. My bad." She grinned, still teasing him. Then she

turned to Grace. "Nice to see you again."

"I'll leave a set of keys for you in an envelope at the Bait & Tackle Co. You can come and go as you please," he said.

"Perfect. I'll get to work." She nodded and waved good-bye. "Hopefully, I'll do such a good job, when I'm done, you'll never know I was here."

Oh. He'd know. He'd know for sure.

Chapter Nine

M ORGAN POURED A cup of coffee and looked around the kitchen. Every inch was cleaned and polished. The counters had been decluttered and the sticky cupboards had been fixed.

Hillcrest House looked better than it had in years after Eli and Dacey spent their free time over Thanksgiving weekend sorting through old family belongings, cleaning up and cleaning out. The idea of living somewhere other than Hillcrest House gave her the jitters, but she conceded selling the big old house wasn't the worst idea ever.

Morgan helped Eli carry his luggage out to the truck. He grabbed the passenger seat moments before her sisters appeared on the front steps. Dacey scrambled into the backseat of the truck, holding her luggage on her lap. Last but not least, Kayla squeezed into the backseat next to her sister for the short drive to the harbor.

"Thank you for all your hard work this weekend," Morgan said, sliding behind the wheel of the truck.

"Are you sure you're cool with putting the house on the market?" Eli asked, studying her face.

Morgan nodded. "But I have one request I'd like to make from all of you."

"What's that?" Eli raised an eyebrow. In the backseat, Kayla and Dacey caught each other's eye.

"One last Christmas in Hillcrest House. All of us. Together." Morgan's voice was flat, but her anxiety made her words tumble out in no particular order.

Eli closed his eyes and let go of a hissing breath. "I'm on board. One hundred percent, Morgan-a."

"Fine by me," Kayla said. "But I have a request too. I want a handmade Christmas."

"Handmade?" Dacey asked. "You actually want me to give you something I made with my own two hands. Are you crazy? I am not crafty."

"I hope you can learn to appreciate the fine art of finger painting." Eli lifted his coffee cup in a salute to his remarkable sisters.

Dacey shook her head. "I'm not sure I'll be able to make it. The year-end is a busy time for us. And my boss told me I had my choice: Thanksgiving or Christmas, but not both. But I swear I will move heaven and earth to be here."

It was the best that Morgan could hope for—everyone agreed to try. She took a deep breath. She needed to celebrate the tiny victory.

Morgan parked the truck in the harbor parking lot.

She grabbed the handle of her sister's luggage and pulled it up and out of the truck bed. During the summer months, the harbor at Christmas Tree Cove was always busy, filled with boats and boaters from all over the Great Lakes. The sailboats returned from Chicago to Mackinac to race. But today a chill wind blew the slushy rain into her face, and every slip in the harbor was empty.

She dragged the suitcase behind her, following Eli and Dacey down to the docks where the amphibious planes were moored. Eli and Dacey checked in for their flight. Morgan helped Skip stow their luggage in the back of the Cessna.

Morgan hugged Eli. "I'll miss having you around the house. You're so loud."

"Don't miss me too much, Morgan-a. I'll be back in a few weeks," he said.

Morgan hugged him tightly. "It was good to see you. Please don't stay away so long again."

Eli took her by the shoulders and looked her in the eyes. "Know your own happiness."

"That's Mom," Kayla said. "Didn't she always say that?"

Morgan smiled. "It's a quote from *Sense and Sensibility.* It was her favorite book."

"Really?" Dacey asked.

Eli laughed. "She made me worry for an entire summer that Marianne was going to fall for Willoughby's bullshit. Don't fall for anyone's bullshit, Morgan-a. No matter what." Morgan nodded and made an attempt to swallow the knot of emotion.

"Hey! I almost forgot," Kayla said. "When we were

cleaning out Mom and Dad's bedroom, we found Mom's jewelry box. We were going to put the contents in a safe-deposit box, but we can't find Grandma's wedding ring. Do either of you know where it is?"

"I have it." Eli raised his hand. "I've always had it. I'll bring it back at Christmas."

Morgan and Kayla stayed on the dock until the small plane took off over the waves of Lake Michigan and then circled back over land. They walked back to the harbor parking lot together.

"Don't stress yourself out too much by making fancy homemade gifts," Kayla said.

Morgan shook her head. "I won't have time. I'm starting a new job." She cleared her throat. "Jesse Taylor hired me to set up a photo gallery in Fish Village."

Kayla looked surprised, uncertain what to say. "What about flying?"

Going to flight school would mean Morgan would have to leave Christmas Tree Cove. She wasn't sure she had the courage to do that. Maybe not ever, but at least not right now. Not when Hillcrest House was being put on the market. She needed to be close to home. "This will keep me in the soup until I start flying charters again in the spring."

"Jesse, huh?" Kayla asked.

"What is that supposed to mean?" Morgan asked.

"He was such a geek when you guys were kids. He's all glowed up. Word around town is he's quite a catch."

Morgan shook her head, careful not to make eye contact. "I'm not fishing."

"That's not what Eli says," Kayla interjected.

Morgan was surprised. "Eli? What did he say?"

"He said that when you were kids, whenever Jesse asked you to play, you always said yes," Kayla said.

"We were good friends."

"'Best friends,' Eli said," Kayla corrected her.

Eli was more aware of her relationship with Jesse than she'd ever guessed. But did he know the truth?

After she said goodbye to Kayla, Morgan picked up the key at the Bait & Tackle Co. and slipped into the gallery. Fumbling for the light switch next to the door, she knocked loose a two-by-four in the open wall. The wood tumbled to the plank floor along with an ancient, sepia-toned photograph.

Morgan was on her hands and knees, studying the old photo she'd found, when Grace suddenly appeared, looking oh-so-stylish in a hunter-green fisherman's knit sweater and dark-washed jeans. "I wanted to pop in and welcome you to the neighborhood. How's it going?"

Morgan stood and walked across the room, holding out the photograph for Grace to see. "I found this in the wall. Do you recognize it?"

"Wow. That's an old one. Maybe even of the first tree in 1918."

"1918? I didn't know the tradition of the floating tree on

Christmas Tree Cove had started so long ago."

"The history of the tree is one of my favorite things." Grace smiled. "It's so romantic."

"Wait. What? I thought the tree was about Christmas and the connection the locals have to the water." Morgan's eyebrows were furrowed. She shrugged to hide her confusion. "How can a Christmas tree be romantic?"

"From the very beginning, the tree was always a floating love story," Grace insisted. "In fact, the very first tree on Christmas Tree Cove was a public acknowledgement of a secret love affair."

Morgan's cheeks prickled with heat. A secret love affair? Seriously? Had Grace guessed she had a past with Jesse Taylor? Had Jesse told her about them? Morgan was even more intrigued than ever. "Seriously? I'm all in."

"It's a featured exhibit in the museum. C'mon, I'll give you a tour."

Grace waited while Morgan locked up the gallery. Morgan followed Grace along the docks to a shanty on the other side of the Bait & Tackle Co.

"A few years ago, the community established a non-profit foundation to preserve Fish Village since it's a living history museum. The old-school jobs in the area—fishing and logging—are disappearing, so we raised enough money to transform an abandoned fish shanty into a place for exhibits and to keep historical archives of Fish Village."

Morgan was grateful for the tour. Grace was so perfectly

coiffed and styled for northern living, and she made Morgan a bit self-conscious about the lack of attention she paid to her own personal appearance.

Grace should be dating Jesse. She's beautiful. He's beautiful. They'd be perfect together.

She wouldn't leave Jesse hanging without any excuse or explanation or avoid speaking to him for six years.

Morgan shoved Jesse's gloves deep into her pockets. She didn't want Grace to recognize them. She should've given them back to Jesse yesterday. She wasn't keeping them because her fingers were cold. She was keeping them because they belonged to him.

"Morgan?" Grace was looking at her quizzically.

Did she say my name more than once?

"I lost you for a moment," Grace said, flashing her warm smile. "Let me guide you."

Morgan followed her to a glass display case. The woman looking back at her from the photograph had her hair pulled back off her face in a no-nonsense style. She had an impish tilt to her lips. Morgan smiled back at her. Here was a woman with grit and determination, much like herself.

"Pauline Nowak was born and grew up here in Christmas Tree Cove. Only in 1918, it was known as Catfish Cove," Grace said.

Morgan scrunched up her nose. "You're kidding."

"Not nearly as romantic as Christmas Tree Cove, is it?" Grace smiled. "Anyway, Pauline went away to school in

Boston and trained as a nurse. In the spring of 1917, she was recruited by the American Red Cross and assigned to a mobile hospital in the Auteuil neighborhood of Paris to tend to Allied soldiers."

Grace pointed to a postcard with a vintage black-and-white photograph of a large canvas tent with Parisian landmarks in the background. "Every day she worked in a makeshift hospital set up in the shadow of the Arc de Triomphe. When the war was over, she sent this postcard to her parents to let them know she was coming home."

The smile on Grace's face held a secret.

"I must be missing something." What did any of this have to do with the floating Christmas tree in the harbor? Or love.

"Here's where the romance begins. She was also the author of this postcard," Grace said, calling Morgan's attention to a postcard had been blown up to poster size. "It was sent to the post office in Juniper Point."

"Juniper Point? On the other side of Sugar Hill?" Morgan asked. She and her sisters had often walked along the beach to the small town in the summer. They had an ice cream stand within walking distance of the beach. It was a few miles from Christmas Tree Cove, and it took a couple of hours to complete the journey, but it wasn't a bad walk. In the summer. On a sunny day.

"Yes, but this was 1918. Back then, Christmas Tree Cove was very isolated. The easiest way to travel in northern

Michigan was by boat. If you wanted to see someone in the next town over during the winter, it was next to impossible. Juniper Point might as well have been located on the other side of Lake Michigan."

Morgan studied the magnified text. The postcard had been written by someone with the same distinctive handwriting as the one the Nowaks had received from their daughter in Paris, obviously written by the same hand in the same old-fashioned, smudged blue ink, with flourishes around the letters F and G. Both postcards had the same cancellation date stamp.

Will be home by Xmas Eve. I await a conspicuous sign of your affections. Otherwise none will be the wiser.

"But no salutation," Morgan noted. "And it's not signed."

"But the handwriting is definitely by the same hand," Grace pointed out.

Swept up in the real-life romance, Morgan's heart was beating faster. "The floating tree was his response to her postcard?" she asked. "A conspicuous sign of affection."

Grace nodded. "A sign of his true devotion, yes."

"Wait. Who was he? Did he grow up here or in Juniper Point?" Morgan asked. Was this guy worthy of this woman she already considered a kindred spirit?

"Pete Blomquist." Grace nodded. "The son of Norwegian immigrants. He worked in his father's boatbuilding shop until he married and moved to Catfish Cove. Pauline was scheduled to arrive home via train on Christmas Eve, but as you know, the weather dictates travel in the winter up here, so we have no idea if she was home in time to see the tree floating in the harbor, but someone did. Whoever the person was who took that photo."

The tiny tree, no more than three feet tall, had been placed in a small wooden dinghy. Its most remarkable feature was the lack of pine needles on its branches, but it was covered with lighted candles.

"If you didn't know all of the story," Morgan said, "you'd make the mistake of claiming that little tree was very unsightly."

"Scrawny," Grace agreed. "Possibly the last one at the tree lot on Christmas Eve."

"But knowing that Pauline came home and found Christmas Tree Cove lit up by this tree just for her . . . Her heart must've exploded with joy when she saw that beautiful little tree.'"

Grace grinned. Her breath caught in her throat. "I can't imagine."

"It's so romantic," Morgan said. "The perfect Christmas gift."

"Not exactly perfect. It did eventually go up in flames." Grace grimaced. "The candles caught the tree and the boat on fire, so nothing remains of the first Christmas display in the harbor, except those two postcards and that photograph."

Morgan sobered. "But it's for certain? Pauline saw the tree? Or heard about it? And they lived happily ever after?"

Grace covered her smile with her hand as she walked across the room to another glass display and pointed to a sepia-toned wedding photograph with a dramatic flourish.

Morgan followed on her heels, taking a step closer to the display. She smiled at the photograph of a group of hearty souls bundled up in warm overcoats and scarves. They were standing on the front steps of the church she'd attended all her life. The same broad wooden doors were decorated with twin pinecone wreaths and long, silver ribbons. In the foreground, two people were nestled together in a one-horse open sleigh.

Pauline's face was calm and serene, with a corsage of winter flowers and a sprig of pine pinned to the front of her heavy woolen coat marking her as the bride. She was tucked under heavy woolen blankets and fur robes in the sleigh.

"They got married," Morgan said, her satisfaction dripping from every syllable. "And lived happily ever after, I hope."

"The man seated next to Pauline in the sleigh is Pete Blomquist," Grace said.

"So he's the one?" Morgan asked.

The bridegroom's smile was wide. Honest. Open. His love for his bride written all over his face.

"Yep. The first guy who put a tree in the harbor."

"For love," Morgan said.

"Isn't that delicious?" Grace asked.

Morgan didn't answer. She was busy studying the wedding photograph.

Pete Blomquist was the only person in the photograph who wasn't looking directly at the camera. His focus was on Pauline, the object of his devotion, his loving glance at his bride captured for all eternity by the photographer.

"Oh. He can't take his eyes off her. How could she ever have doubted his constancy?" Morgan said, wiping away a tear with a tissue quickly handed to her by Grace.

"For the next forty years, a time spanning three generations, the Blomquist family took responsibility for putting out a lighted tree in the harbor every year on Christmas Eve. Which is why we grew up in a place called Christmas Tree Cove, instead of Catfish Cove."

Morgan laughed.

Grace smiled. "Pete and Pauline Blomquist bought land north of town, where he planted most of the pine forest that still covers Sugar Hill. They lived in the house on Hill Street where she was born and raised eight children."

"Eight?" Morgan asked.

"Winters are long in northern Michigan." Grace laughed.

Morgan stepped back from the display. "How did you ever come across this story?"

"We try to collect correspondence from local families. They are a great resource of local history," Grace said. "A boat builder from Muskegon donated some of his family's old letters and photographs.

"Nels Blomquist?" Morgan asked. His name was a part of her own family history. "He built *Faith* for my great-grandfather."

"He's Pete and Pauline's grandson. The Blomquist family claims responsibility for the tree's appearance in the harbor on Christmas Eve through the late fifties. It's a bit of a mystery about who continued the tradition. We have photos of the floating trees in our archives, but no claims of responsibility, even though the floating tree made its final appearance six years ago."

"I hate that the floating tree is now a part of Christmas Tree Cove history."

"Me too." Grace nodded.

"Thank you for showing me the exhibit," Morgan said, pulling on her jacket. "Is it possible to get a digital image of the first tree? Jesse has so many photographs of the tree on Christmas Tree Cove from over the years. It would make an amazing window display for the gallery."

"That's a great idea. If you get anyone to confess or come across any good photos, let me know."

"You've given me a good mystery to solve." Morgan grinned.

"I'm glad to know someone one who's as fascinated with the history of Christmas Tree Cove as I am."

Morgan nodded. Whether or not she was dating Jesse,

Grace was kind and gracious—a good person to have as a friend in a place as small as Christmas Tree Cove. "Since I'll be working in the gallery most days, let me know if you ever want to grab lunch."

Grace flashed a warm smile. "Actually, I'd really love that."

Morgan stepped out onto the dock and turned her collar up to the cold breeze off the lake. She would find out more about the floating Christmas tree. How many hands had been involved in the Christmas Eve spectacle over the years? Who put out the tree while she was growing up? At the very least, she wanted to know who had put out the last tree in the harbor—the one floating on Christmas Tree Cove the night her parents died.

Chapter Ten

JESSE NEEDED TO finish setting up these shots before he lost the light. And he needed to keep from losing his temper every time the clueless art director gave him notes.

Smile and nod.

It's a freelance assignment. It's not forever.

He talked to Matt Wendell again. He was still on the fence about the job. It was a corporate position, and he wasn't sure he was cut out to work in an office, but the offer was more money than Jesse had ever dreamed of making. But money had never been his top priority and New York City was feeling less like home.

Especially since Morgan texted almost once an hour from Christmas Tree Cove, not with questions but with choices. Paint samples. Floor coverings. Lighting options. Frame and matte colors. The options were endless. He'd had no idea how many decisions needed to be made in order to get the gallery up and running. She sent photos and specific examples, proving to be as detail-oriented as he was. They quickly developed a shorthand, most often responding to each other in a series of emojis.

He could get used to this lifestyle. Being away from home working on freelance assignment wasn't as lonely when he was getting text messages from her at all hours of the day and night. It would be even more fun if she could travel with him to all the places his work took him.

Don't do it. Don't let your imagination run away with you.

Their current situation was not a long-term solution to his problems. Or hers. She would need to move on and find a job that was better suited for her. They were just friends. Anything more would be playing with fire. He hoped this time, he wasn't the one who got burned.

And yet. All he wanted was to go back to Christmas Tree Cove. He told himself he needed to check on all the changes Morgan was making at the gallery, but the truth was, he wanted to see her.

Jesse was on his way over to the gallery in Fish Village after disembarking from the three-thirteen when he ran smack into her coming around the corner of the docks with lunch in her hands. They clung to each other for a moment. His free hand knocked his wheeled suitcase into the lake with a loud splash, and the case began drifting slowly away.

Morgan ran over to the edge of the dock. She looked prepared to dive into the water. "Is any of your photographic equipment in that bag?"

He shook his head. "No."

"Is it waterproof?"

"I guess we'll find out, won't we?" This was not the reunion he'd planned in his imagination. Not even close.

Morgan raised her eyebrows. "Do you want some help?

"I've got this." He stretched out his full length on the dock and reached for the suitcase. It was a few inches beyond his hands. He reached forward, and suddenly a larger fraction of his body was dangling dangerously over water than was supported by the dock. He made a small sound.

"I'm not a strong swimmer," Jesse said.

Without hesitation, Morgan laid down on the dock next to him and wrapped herself around his waist in a giant bear hug. He stiffened at her touch. "What are you doing?"

"Making sure you don't fall in," she said, forcing a smile.

She tucked her head under his chin, and he inhaled her scent as if she were an expensive glass of wine.

Putting his long arms to good use, he stretched forward to reach again for the suitcase bobbing in the water, the movement pulling her with him toward the edge of the dock.

For a moment he was certain they were both going to end up in the water, until he finally managed to pull the suitcase close enough to snag it with his fingertips. He pulled it closer to the dock.

Morgan untangled herself from him and scrambled upright just as Jesse swung the suitcase onto dock with a bit too much extra force. He accidentally knocked his glasses clear off his face.

Morgan found them a few yards away on the dock and passed them back to Jesse.

"Thank you." Pressing one finger to the bridge of the frames, he pushed them back up on his face. It was a gesture he'd been performing since elementary school.

"When did you get in?" she asked.

"I just landed."

"You didn't tell me you were coming back. I'm flying a couple of hunters up to St. Ignace or else I'd stay and chat, but I'm looking forward to your feedback on the window display."

"I'll have to check it out."

"Can I ask you a personal question?" Morgan asked.

He nodded, even though he wasn't sure he wanted to hear her question.

"Are you dating Grace?"

Jesse rubbed the back of his neck. "It's nice that the gossip grapevine of Christmas Tree Cove has been so kind as to insert me into the narrative when they're making up stories, but I am not dating Grace. She's seeing a really nice guy, a financial planner from Grand Rapids. She wants to move away from Christmas Tree Cove more than anything."

"Oh," Morgan said. A long, awkward moment passed between them. "I really like her."

"Me too," Jesse said. *But I like you more.* He left those words unspoken.

Morgan looked up at the sky. He followed her gaze. Dark clouds were gathering on the horizon. "There's a storm coming," he said.

She nodded. "A big one. And soon."

Then she walked away and turned onto the path to the harbor without another word.

Chapter Eleven

J UST AS MORGAN and Jesse had predicted Christmas Tree Cove was getting the kind of precipitation that defied description by one word alone. Slush. Freezing rain. The roads were like ice skating rinks, making driving treacherous.

Morgan took her time walking on the icy docks in Fish Village. She'd flown two planeloads of hunters and all their gear out to the islands before sunup. The plane wasn't heated and even in her Carhartt overalls and jacket, she was cold through to her bones.

All she wanted was a cup of coffee.

Morgan pushed open the door of Bait & Tackle Co. and was immediately overcome by a sickly stench. She nearly gagged.

Burnt sugar. Cinnamon . . . and quite possibly human hair.

Morgan covered her face with her hand to keep from inhaling the acrid smoke. Whatever it was—and it was terrible—was the reason a cloud of smoke hanging near the ceiling in the two-story eating area.

"Hello," Morgan called.

No one was behind the counter. The kitchen looked empty too. She stepped behind the counter and peeked further into the kitchen. No one was in sight.

She walked into the kitchen.

Aurora was huddled on the floor near the convection oven. Far from her usual role as a style maven, her hair had fallen out of her messy bun. Flour and bits of charcoal streaked across on her nose.

"Did something or somebody catch on fire?" Morgan asked.

"I burned two trays of rolls." Aurora said. She wiped her face with a paper towel. Morgan stepped over Jesse's sister and opened the back door, propping it open to allow some of the black smoke out. Hopefully, it would also let in some air that was actually breathable.

"What happened?" Morgan asked, dropping to her knees.

Aurora wiped tears off her face, but her cheeks were still streaked with mascara and her eyes were swollen and red. "After I burned the rolls and forgot to make pizza dough, I completely spaced on the order for the Juniper Point Garden Club Christmas luncheon."

"You've got to get on that," Morgan said in a good-natured way. "The Garden Club ladies can be mean."

"Super mean," Aurora emphasized with a grin.

"Is that everything on your current list of problems?" Morgan asked.

Aurora nodded.

"Okay. Let's get a new tray of rolls in the oven. I'll make some coffee. You're going to be fine."

A half an hour later, Morgan unlocked the gallery and turned on the lights. Jesse had gone out of town again on assignment, but she was pleased with the situation in the gallery. The electricians had finished hanging the lighting tracks. She'd ordered rugs to put out on the wooden floors. And she was getting close to having everything hung on the walls. She needed to focus on the computerized inventory system as soon as the hardware arrived.

She was up on a ladder hanging the gallery sign over the wrap stand when Jesse's mom came through the door, holding an open umbrella and carrying a paper bag.

"I brought rolls to thank you for rescuing Aurora," she said.

"Thank you. That's so sweet," Morgan said, climbing down off the ladder.

Mrs. Taylor unzipped her jacket and walked around the room. "You've done an amazing job with the place. I never doubted you for a minute, but I wasn't sure if Jesse had brought you in because of your organizational skills or because he assumed you'd scare me away."

Morgan spit out her coffee. She never expected Jesse's mom to be so honest. "It's probably fifty-fifty."

"I'll bet," she said. "I suspect he actually answers your text messages."

Morgan paused. "Not always. But most days, he's pretty prompt."

"The next time you hear from him, will you tell him to make sure he waters the Christmas tree at our house while we're in Florida?"

"You're going to Florida?" Morgan asked.

"For Christmas," she nodded. "We're taking Aurora and flying out over the weekend."

"What about Jesse and Pops?"

"Jesse can't make up his mind. Some days he says he'll come to Florida with us. Other days he says he can't spend the holidays anywhere other than Christmas Tree Cove. He's going to stay behind and look after Pops. Honestly, I think it's the other way around."

Morgan held an awkward smile on her face. She didn't know the Jesse who'd go to Florida for Christmas. Her Jesse would want to be in Christmas Tree Cove this time of year.

She wanted to text Jesse the message from his mom immediately, anticipating his reaction, but instead she climbed back up the ladder.

Jesse's mom opened the door to leave but paused. "I really liked your mom, Morgan. We talked about our kids a lot. She wanted to give you roots so you would know who you are. But she wanted to make sure you had wings, so you could fly and become whatever your heart desired."

Morgan smiled. "That's why I became a pilot."

"I'm not sure flying amphibious airplanes for Skip Brunell was what your mom had in mind. She really wanted you to soar."

Tears pressed against the back of Morgan's eyes. Jesse's mom was the last person on earth she wanted to see her cry.

"I know you feel safe right now, tucked away in Fish Village," she said. "But your mom wouldn't want you to delay your dreams again."

Morgan nodded. "Thanks for telling me. I appreciate it. Very much."

Jesse's mom picked up her umbrella, and in a heartbeat, she was gone.

Morgan closed her eyes. Jesse's mom was right, she needed to find a way to fly. Skip always told that he would help her go back to flight school, but she had so much to do in Christmas Tree Cove. She had promised Jesse she'd set up the gallery. And with Hillcrest House on the market, she'd have to clear it out when it sold.

There were so many reasons to stay. And yet, her heart told her she needed to leave. This was the perfect time.

If only Jesse wasn't so busy trying to find his way back to Christmas Tree Cove when she was trying to find her way to fly away. How would he ever understand?

We were in love.

He'd said the words without hesitation.

Six years had gone by and hearing him say those four words made her heart flutter and rendered her speechless. Her cheeks flushed hot.

Love.

She measured every man she ever met against him. She didn't mean to. It just happened. No one was as tall as Jesse. No one made her laugh as hard as Jesse. No one made her as mad as Jesse.

Could we build a life together? Or are we destined to live apart?

Morgan was working on inventory when the door opened again, and Kayla strolled in. She'd been hoping for a surprise visit from Jesse, but her sister was almost as nice.

"I can't believe this is Obermeyer's old shanty," she said, taking in the two-story ceiling.

Morgan nodded. "It's amazing, isn't it? It's all Jesse."

Standing close to the window, Kayla wrinkled her nose. "What is that smell?"

"It's my jacket. I put it over the heater to dry."

Kayla snuck up on the jacket hanging over the heat register. She made a face. "That's it."

Morgan shrugged. "I don't notice it as much when I'm in an unheated plane."

"Is this your only warm coat?" Dacey asked. "And where did you get the gloves?"

"Jesse gave them to me," Morgan responded honestly.

Kayla made a face. "They smell worse than the jacket."

"They're a loan and may've been frequently used to clean fish."

Kayla tossed the gloves down on the floor. "Do you plan

on working here long-term?"

"Jesse and I haven't made any kind of long-term arrangement. This gig is strictly temporary."

"Are we still talking about a job?" Kayla asked.

"I-I don't have any other kind of relationship with Jesse," Morgan stammered.

"Okay. Let's table that for a moment," she said. "Here's the thing. As long as you are working in a retail environment and you're planning a grand opening gala, it might be a good time to spruce up your wardrobe a bit."

"I hate shopping," Morgan said, making a face.

"Humor me," Kayla said. "And if you're well-behaved, I'll buy you wine."

Morgan took a deep breath. She'd stop shopping for anything new for herself. Over the last six years, most of her purchases had been for Hillcrest House. She needed to refresh her style, and some clothes might be the right place to start. Mrs. Taylor's words echoed in her head.

She wanted you to soar.

"All right," she said. "I'll do it. But I'm not giving up my Carhartt jacket until spring thaw."

SHE AND KAYLA took the one women's boutique in Christmas Tree Cove by storm. Morgan bought wool pants and sweater separates in dark shades of gray and black. She could mix and match them with her jeans. Kayla insisted she try on a dark green sheath dress that made her feel like a glittering Christmas ornament.

"You have to wear that for the gallery opening," Kayla said.

Morgan nodded. The dress fit her like a dream.

"It's nice to see you investing in yourself," Kayla said. "Avoiding life is not an option."

"I'm not avoiding life. I'm not a people person."

"I'm not going to argue with you. Not when you're in such a good mood," Kayla said. "Let's stop off at the hair salon next."

Morgan was having too much fun with Kayla to voice any objections.

Two hours later, Morgan walked down River Street feeling like a princess. The stylist had cut long layers in her dark hair and added highlights of gold and amber. Kayla insisted on putting Morgan's salon visit on her credit card, which made her fidgety with guilt.

But Kayla wasn't hearing any of it. "Remember what Mom always said when any of us started to throw a pity party."

"Count your blessings. Write them down. Make a list. Number them," Morgan said.

"Even when the worst happens," Kayla added.

"FYI. You're in my top five," Morgan said.

"You're in mine," Kayla grinned.

"Look, there's Grace," Morgan said, waving to Grace, who was walking up the hill from the harbor. "You were friends with her in high school, weren't you?"

Kayla nodded. "She's really nice, but Jesse is *the* sugar plum dancing through the long winter's-night dreams of the ladies in Christmas Tree Cove," Kayla said. "Are they dating?"

Morgan shook her head. "I've got it on good authority."

"Good to know," Grace said.

They waited on the corner for Grace to catch up with them. "What are you guys doing?"

"We've been shopping," Kayla said.

"I was promised wine if I was on my best behavior," Morgan reminded her. "We're on our way to The Sip. Do you want to join us?"

Grace grinned. "Sounds like a good time."

By the time they got to Main Street, the sky was getting darker as the rain turned into snow. The sidewalks were covered in a slippery combination of sleet. Morgan, Grace, and Kayla pulled and tugged each other into the middle of the street. The snowplows hadn't been by to clear the roads yet, but there weren't many cars out, and they had Main Street to themselves. Their joyful laughter echoed through the streets of Christmas Tree Cove.

In the company of Grace and Kayla, Morgan's mood was suddenly buoyant. She wasn't sure what her future held, but it didn't matter. Tonight, she was going to have fun.

Chapter Twelve

WHEN THE DIVE bar at the corner of Main Street and Harbor changed hands right after the Christmas holidays ten years ago, the new owner left the decorations up well into the spring. The cherry blossoms were blooming in the nearby orchards, and there was still a life-sized Santa waving from a plastic chimney on the roof of the bar in Christmas Tree Cove. And in a blink of an eye, the beach bar originally known as The Sip Shack became Santa's Sip Shack.

The Sip, as it was called by the locals, hadn't been redecorated in years. The food was good and so was the selection of local beer and wine. Most days it was more like a community center than a watering hole, especially in the winter, when the days were short and the nights were long.

"Three glasses of your house red."

Jesse turned at the sound of Morgan's voice. What was she doing here? She wasn't a part of the local crowd who hung out at The Sip. Not now. Not ever.

She returned to the table where she was seated with her sister and Grace. He stared at Morgan for a long time. She didn't notice him. Or if she did, she didn't betray any outward signs of recognition.

He'd been away for ten days, and in that time, the gallery had been completely transformed. With his blessing, she'd hung a sign out over the docks. She'd picked out paint and floor coverings. She'd decorated the front window and chosen the photographs to feature in the advertising.

Her most recent text included plans for a gala grand opening of the gallery two days before Christmas. She had even gotten his mother involved in making the appetizers. He wouldn't care if it was only him and Pops sitting around in the gallery on opening night, but she had big plans. All of Christmas Tree Cove was invited. Her enthusiasm was infectious.

And nearly everyone he'd run into since he'd gotten home had told him that they planned on being there.

Jesse took a long pull from the glass in front of him on the counter. It cooled all the way down to his toes. He wasn't at The Sip to socialize; he wanted to have a beer and unwind. But he figured he should at least say hello.

Before he had a chance to say a word of greeting, Morgan shouted to the bartender, "Hey, Russell. Where did you get these photos of the floating Christmas tree?"

As the only full-time bartender at The Sip, Russell Wiggs had plenty of time for his two favorite hobbies: spreading gossip and flirting.

"They've been there forever."

"Seriously?" she asked.

"Hiding in plain sight."

"They're pretty old." She was pressed against the wall, studying the photographs. God, she was beautiful. It had been so long since he'd seen her with all her hair falling in a loose, dark cloud down her back.

"Who do they belong to?" she asked.

"My uncle Fermin." Russell walked out from behind the bar to join Morgan along the wall. "He ran the postal boat that serviced the islands. Back then, all the islands still had small family farms. He fell in love with one of the girls on the island. My aunt Adelaide. When she moved into town, he started putting out the tree in the harbor for her."

Morgan nodded. "Of course he did. Because it was always about true love."

Russell smiled. "Yep. She was homesick for an island Christmas."

"How long did he do it?" she asked.

"Put the tree out in the harbor? Gosh, I'm not sure exactly." Russell paused for a moment. "Long time. Until she died sometime in the late fifties, I guess."

"Grace?" Morgan waved her over. "Have you seen these photos?"

She joined Morgan at the photo wall. Jesse took another sip of his beer, trying to ignore Russell, who was turning himself inside out, catering to the needs of the two women peppering him with questions.

"Is that tinsel?" Grace asked, pointing to one of the photographs on the wall.

"Yep," Russell said, ignoring his duties behind the bar. "He used colored lights and car batteries to keep them on all night."

"On a dive raft?" Morgan asked.

"Actually. It was a shipping pallet," he said. "Cheaper than a dive raft, but more likely to sink."

It wasn't long before Grace and Morgan were absorbed in the photos, hanging on Russell's every word. Jesse wasn't sure how much longer he could stay while Russell attempted to flirt with two women at the same time. It made him queasy. Especially when one of them was Morgan.

"These are amazing," Grace said. "I've never seen photos of the tree from this era before."

"Me neither," Morgan said. "We could put all the vintage photos of the floating tree together on one poster and sell them as a fundraiser for the museum at the grand opening."

"That would be awesome," Grace agreed.

"I'll have to check through Jesse's files, but I'm pretty sure he has some photographs from the last few years the tree was put out in the harbor. But will we have time to get them printed for the opening of the gallery?" Morgan wondered out loud.

That was the last straw. Morgan was talking about the gallery—his gallery—as if he wasn't a factor in it. As if he were invisible. It was okay when they were kids, but now that they were grown-ups, it was too much.

When Morgan and Grace walked back to where Kayla was seated, Jesse took it as his opportunity to join the conversation. He carried his beer over to their table.

"Hi," he said, sitting down without waiting for an invitation.

"Jesse," Morgan said, acting surprised to see him. "You remember my sister Kayla, don't you? She's the new art teacher at the elementary school."

"Really? Art was my favorite class," Jesse said.

Kayla smiled. "I put up with such an unreasonably high level of cuteness. Sometimes I don't think I'll make it through another day. Especially this time of year."

Her enthusiasm was charming. Jesse smiled warmly. "It's good to see you again."

Russell appeared with three glasses of wine on a tray. He set them down in front of each woman. "Put their drinks on my tab," Jesse said.

"You don't have to do that," Morgan protested.

Kayla put her hand over her sister's hand to stop her. "Say 'thank you,' Morgan."

"Thank you," Morgan said.

"Please forgive her," Kayla said. "She doesn't get out much."

"But this is supposed to be single ladies' night out," Grace protested.

"I don't mind if Jesse joins us," Kayla said.

"But it's not an official 'single ladies' night out if there's a guy sitting at our table," Grace insisted.

Jesse turned to Morgan for support. "You're kidding, right?"

Morgan shrugged. "I was promised wine."

Grace shook her head. Her eyes sparkled with mirth. "That's the rules on ladies' night out. We're all single and ready to mingle. No dudes. Are you sure you still want to buy us drinks?"

"Wait," Jesse said, looking at Grace. "You're not single. You're dating that guy from . . ."

"Grand Rapids," Grace said.

He pointed at Kayla. "You're married to the deputy sheriff." Then he looked at Morgan. "And you're . . ." he stopped himself. Morgan stared up at him, challenging him with her eyes.

"Super single," Kayla said. "And I didn't pay one hundred and fifty bucks for her highlights for her to sit around Hillcrest House every night watching K-dramas all by herself. She's the reason we're here."

Morgan took a sip of her wine. Her cheeks were pink with embarrassment, but she didn't contradict her sister. Jesse drained the last of his beer and slammed the glass down on the tabletop. "I'm out."

He grabbed his jacket off the back of his stool and nodded to the barkeep. "I'm buying their first round."

His long strides took him out the front door in a matter of seconds. He crossed the parking lot and opened the door to his truck before her voice stopped him in his tracks.

"Jesse, wait up a second." He hesitated for a moment. He was playing with fire. It was one thing to admit to himself that he still had feelings for her. It was another thing to go public with his feelings. He wasn't ready for this. Not by a long shot.

Morgan traced his footsteps to where he had left his truck in the far corner of the parking lot. She grimaced. "I'm sorry."

He shrugged. "What happened in there?"

"It's single ladies' night out." She sighed. "We never discussed how we were supposed to behave in public with each other."

"It's not a secret. People know we know each other," he said.

"And that I'm working in your gallery. It shouldn't be so awkward between us."

They were standing very close together in a dark corner of the parking lot. Without her coat, she huddled closer to him for warmth with the sweetest smile on her face.

"Nobody knows that we broke each other's hearts when we were younger," she said.

"You broke my heart," he insisted. He was the injured party.

She grimaced. "I don't want to fight with you."

Jesse let go of a deep breath. "Let's move on. I'm sorry if I made it awkward in The Sip."

"I was feeling awkward too," she admitted. "I don't usually come to places like this. I'm not certain how to behave."

Without a word, he reached for her, pulling her close to him. Morgan took a step forward, a smile on her parted lips. He cupped her cheek in his hand. Running the tips of his rough fingers along the line of her chin, he mapped out a path to her mouth.

"Jesse," she said.

"Witch's eyes," he murmured under his breath.

His lips brushed hers. Her lips were softer than he remembered, touching his like a whisper, her warm, sweet breath on him. His lips were hard and searching. Her tongue traced the softness of his lips. A gasp of pleasure escaped her, then his mouth covered hers hungrily. Pleasure radiated out through his body to his fingers and toes. He didn't remember their kisses being like this—so completely consuming—but they must've been. He was no longer sure of time and space. It was as if they were kissing inside a dreamy winter wonderland of their own.

Her lips curled into a smile against his, then she rested her head on his shoulder. Jesse took a deep breath, attempting to calm his heartbeat that was echoing loudly in his ears.

He pulled her closer, holding her against the length of his body. For the first time in as long as he could remember, he was exactly where he wanted to be at exactly the right time.

"I've got an early flight in the morning." He kissed her on the forehead. "I'll miss you," he breathed into her ear. The words dropped out of his mouth and he held his breath. Waited for her response. She didn't lift her head from his shoulder. Her breath tickled the hollow between his neck and shoulder.

"I'll miss you more," she said so softly he wasn't sure she'd said them out loud. Then she turned and walked back into the bar.

Chapter Thirteen

December 20

M ORGAN WAS LOST in a world of her own. Her hands were jammed deeply into her pockets as she crossed the street in front of Hillcrest House. The For Sale sign on the front lawn was an unnecessary reminder her reality was changing faster than she could cope. Yet putting Hillcrest House on the market wasn't what was occupying her thoughts.

The kiss.

It had been one week since they'd kissed, and it was still on her mind. They fit together perfectly, like two pieces of a puzzle that had finally come together after a very long time apart in the bottom of a box.

In the graying light of dusk, snow clouds were gathering far off on the horizon of Lake Michigan. Morgan had always been able to feel a snowstorm in her bones, like her mom. She paused long enough to take a deep breath. Christmas Tree Cove smelled of fresh lake water, balsam and cedarwood.

His soft lips. The tickle of his beard. His ice-blue eyes.

A moment later she was sprawled across the snowy ground, flat on her back. Complete wipe out. Felled by an icy patch underneath the snow. Her emotions were as scattered and shaken as she was. She scrambled to her feet and dusted off the snow.

"I kissed Jesse," she said. "What was I thinking?"

She paused momentarily, waiting for a response from her mom. Instead, the voice inside her head answered.

Of course it's Jesse. No one will ever compare to your first love. Let it go, Morgan. It doesn't mean anything. Not to him.

And it shouldn't mean anything to her either. She didn't need to make a habit of kissing random people. Especially people who were providing her with a paycheck for the next three months.

She closed her eyes. All she could see was Jesse. His wide mouth. His warm eyes.

Kissing Jesse. Stop.

She wasn't aware she had walked up the steps of the Kimuras' front door. "Stop," she said. Mrs. Kimura opened the door faster than Morgan was expecting, surprising them both. "Kissing Jesse."

"What?" Mrs. Kimura asked.

"Nothing." Morgan's cheeks flushed.

"Oh, Morgan. I'm so glad you're here," she said with a smile in her voice as she ushered her through the front door. "We heard you're working in Fish Village."

She nodded. "I'm setting up Jesse Taylor's fine arts photography gallery."

"How do you like working for Jesse?"

"Kissing," Morgan responded with the first word that popped into her mind.

Mrs. Kimura's sharp, indrawn breath brought Morgan back to reality. "You kissed Jesse Taylor? I'll put the kettle on. Tell me everything. Spare no detail."

"Wait!" Morgan followed her into the kitchen, where Mrs. Kimura moved quickly to put the teakettle onto a burner and fill an infuser ball with loose tea leaves. "What did I say?" Morgan asked.

"You said you'd been kissing Jesse Taylor."

"No. Not kissing," Morgan protested, making an exaggerated "ick face" to sell her lies. "Not me. Not Jesse. I was sorting through some of the recent photographs he's taken for clients. A surprise proposal. Out at the lighthouse. It was very sweet. Kissing. It's been on my mind."

"Rii-iight," Mrs. Kimura said. "Well. Let's have some tea. I'm sure we'll figure out something else to chat about."

Morgan wasn't sure Mrs. Kimura was completely buying her lies. She really needed to focus on something other than Jesse.

Or kissing.

"I want to show you something." Mrs. Kimura led her out onto a three-season porch overlooking her garden. Every flat surface was filled with little glass jars.

Morgan's heart leaped at the sight. "The Christmas terrariums. You started without me."

"I thought you'd get a kick out of seeing them. Your mom and I used to pull all-nighters to get them made and ready for delivery the day before Christmas Eve. Now I know better. I start a month in advance."

Morgan laughed. "It may sound like the beginning of a scary fairytale, but Mom used to drive us up to Sugar Hill and send Kayla and me out into the pine forest to scavenge for winterberries."

Mrs. Kimura wagged a finger. "Totally illegal. I have to order winterberries from online suppliers now. They're very expensive. But everyone loves them so much. Your mom and I would fill the backseat of her station wagon and drive all over the countryside, delivering them to retirement homes, assisted living facilities, and elderly shut-ins scattered throughout the county." She lifted the lid off a terrarium and held it out for Morgan. "What does it smell like?"

Moss. Minty winterberries. Evergreen balsam. The scent instantly made Morgan homesick for Christmases past. "Christmas Tree Cove under glass," she said with a wistful smile.

"We were so lucky when your family moved in across the street," Mrs. Kimura said. "Our hearts were broken when the For Sale sign went up."

Morgan shook her head. "Mom always said we were the lucky ones. To have you as our neighbors."

Mrs. Kimura shook her head. "Your mom needed help in

the worst way. She was running the shop down in the harbor and had three very active kids on her hands. I offered to babysit. I didn't know what I was doing, but you were so willing to hang out in the garden. Dig in the dirt. Water the flowers. Such a gentle child."

Morgan snorted. "You're probably the only person on earth who has ever described me as gentle." Impulsive? Opinionated? Yes. Gentle? Hardly ever.

"You always reserved your anger for those who deserved it."

"Not always," Morgan conceded. More than once, she'd fought with Jesse because he never put up much of fight. He let her have her way.

"I spent the summers in your garden, and the winters on the ice rink while Kayla and Dacey took ballet," Morgan said. "Jesse taught me how to skate."

"Really?" Mrs. Kimura asked, the one word heavily laced with innuendo.

Morgan side-eyed her. "The only reason Jesse Taylor taught me to skate was because he and his friends needed a goalie. They used me for target practice."

"Why are you blushing?" Mrs. Kimura asked.

"I'm not." Morgan's protest was completely ineffective. The heat had traveled up her neck and filled her cheeks. "Kayla inherited Mom's grace. She never stumbles or takes a false step. She looks as if she's floating above the ground. Dacey has Mom's tenacity and determination."

"But you are your mom in so many ways," Mrs. Kimura said.

Morgan shook her head. "I'm more of a blend of Mom and Dad."

Mrs. Kimura shook her head. "Your personality may be like your dad, but you look like her. And that's a very good thing."

Morgan followed Mrs. Kimura back out to the kitchen where they were settled at the kitchen table with steaming mugs when Mr. Kimura came through the front door, stomping snow off his boots.

"We're getting a storm," he said.

Morgan nodded. "It's gonna be a snow bomb."

Mrs. Kimura gestured to the table. "Look who dropped in."

"I'm so glad you're here," Mr. Kimura said with a grin. "She only brings out the good treats for company." He pulled a mug out of the cupboard and poured tea for himself.

"That's not true." Mrs. Kimura said, carrying a plate of treats to the table. She passed them to Morgan.

"What are these?"

"Salted caramel brownies," she said. "Two tastes that don't belong together at first glance, but in reality, enhance the flavor of the other."

Is that Jesse and me?

"Try one," Mr. Kimura said.

"They're delicious." Morgan said.

"We were so glad to hear you found a job," he said. "We were worried we let you down by keeping the shop closed over the winter."

Morgan leaned forward and touched Mr. Kimura's hand. "Please don't worry about me. I'm going to be fine."

"What will you do when the house sells?" he asked. "Will you keep flying charters for Skip? Have you considered the pilot training program again?"

"I don't know if I can qualify. Every plane has its own personality. The de Havilland I've been flying is basically a vintage pick up. Will I be able to make the switch to a plane that's like a race car?" Morgan asked. "Who knows? And I haven't had time to think beyond Christmas."

"Take your time," Mrs. Kimura whispered. "This could be the last Adair Christmas in Hillcrest House. You have to make it special."

"Right now, I'm keeping my fingers crossed that Dacey can make it. She's still uncertain. More than anything else, I want to be together as a family. Otherwise, all the fairy lights and glitter in the world won't mean a thing."

Mrs. Kimura smiled. "Truer words were never spoken."

"I should get going." Morgan stood. Her departure was halted by a vintage photograph of the floating Christmas tree in the harbor on the wall in the hallway. In the image, the tree was taller than she remembered, with colored lights, and was floating on a dive raft.

"Did Jesse Taylor take this?" she asked.

Mrs. Kimura glanced at her husband. A spark of some indefinable emotion flashed in her eyes. "No. It's from much earlier."

"Really? I've been looking for photos of the earlier trees ever since I visited the museum exhibit about the first tree in the harbor. Turns out a relative of Russell Wiggs put out the tree for his wife in the fifties, but no one seems to want to take credit for putting the tree out in recent years."

Mrs. Kimura turned from the sink, wiping her hands on a dish towel. She glanced at her husband, then cleared her throat. "When we first moved here, I wasn't so sure I liked living in the north woods. I was from San Francisco. I was very urbane and sophisticated. Too much for a small town."

She touched her hair in a dramatic display of sophistication, making Morgan grin.

"I hoped the tree would welcome her to Christmas Tree Cove. So she'd know she was home," Mr. Kimura said. "But I dragged that tree out into the harbor every Christmas Eve for nearly twenty years before she figured it out."

Mrs. Kimura laughed, looking at her husband with pure love and devotion. "Crazy man."

"When was this?" Morgan asked.

"From the late seventies until the early nineties."

"Who was putting out the tree before you did it?"

Mr. Kimura was quiet for a moment. "When we first moved to Christmas Tree Cove, if I remember correctly, it was one of Skip Brunell's relatives who was putting out the tree."

"Skip? Seriously?" Morgan shook her head. "I never would've asked him about it."

"I'm pretty sure it was one of his uncles who inherited the honor of putting out the tree," Mr. Kimura said.

"The honor?" Morgan grinned. "Seems a bit dubious."

"Through the eyes of a child, I'm sure the tree was nothing more than a magical holiday decoration. But hearing all the stories about the floating tree, it's very clear it was always an act of love," Mrs. Kimura smiled.

"And hope."

Mr. Kimura chuckled. "You had to have a pretty good reason to do it. Wrestling a lighted Christmas tree onto a boat in the middle of winter isn't all fun and games."

Morgan laughed. "Did my mom know about the tree and its connection to true love?"

"I'm sure she did." Mrs. Kimura smiled.

Morgan's breath caught in her throat. This new information about the tree filled her with a warm glow. She found her iPhone in her coat pocket and checked the time. "I should go."

Mrs. Kimura followed her out onto the front porch. "Listen. I don't want to interfere with your work at the gallery, but if you want to join me in delivering the terrariums on Christmas Eve, I'd love the company."

"The grand opening is the night before Christmas Eve,

so I'll be free. No matter what," Morgan said. "Hey. Is it possible to get a digital copy of that photo?" Morgan paused on the front steps. "I want to show it to Grace."

"I'll tell Mr. Kimura to forward you a copy," she said, waving goodbye.

Morgan left the Kimuras' house feeling buoyant. She could hardly wait to talk to Skip.

Chapter Fourteen

J ESSE WALKED THROUGH the front door of the gallery and stopped. Skip was holding one of his framed photographs up to the wall. Morgan stood a few feet away, judging by eye to see if it was level.

"What are you doing here?" Jesse asked, nodding in Skip's general direction. "You should know better. If you get within five yards of here, she'll put you to work."

Skip nodded. "She left me a message, so I hurried right over. The next thing I know, I've got a hammer and some nails in my hands."

"It's called multitasking. You guys should try it," Morgan said. "I called you because I heard your uncle was one of the guys who put the tree out in the harbor on Christmas Eve."

Skip nodded. "My Uncle Marshall. He did it for many years."

"Was he trying to woo a girl?" Jesse asked.

"In a way, you could say so." Skip's tone was more sober than usual. "Uncle Marshall was a widower. His wife died many years before he did. Christmas was her favorite time of year. So every year after she passed on, he put the tree in the harbor as a memorial to her."

Morgan took a sharp intake of breath. "Does your family have any photos of that tree?"

"Maybe. In an old photo album. I can check later tonight." Skip shrugged. "I've got to run to do the three-thirteen." As he slipped into his coat, he turned to Jesse. "You're back early. Thought you weren't due until the weekend."

"I caught the morning flight, but it wasn't the same without you," Jesse said with a grin.

"I'll get going," Skip said, moving toward the door. He looked back at Morgan. "Keep me posted about the flight to Chicago. I can set something up."

"Will do," Morgan said. "Call me if you find any old pics of your Uncle Marshall's tree." She picked up another framed photograph, carrying it to a blank spot on the wall. "How does it look?"

"The place looks great," Jesse said, taking a brief glance around the room. The shack he'd spent so long rebuilding had been completely transformed. "You've done an amazing job."

Morgan and Jesse worked together in the gallery for the next few hours. The next time Jesse looked up, the sun had already set, but Morgan was still busy on her laptop. "Are you doing anything for dinner?"

"Are you asking me on a date?" Morgan looked him straight in the eye.

Jesse laughed uncomfortably. "No. Not a date. Don't be ridiculous." His mouth was so dry, his lips kept sticking to his teeth. Of course he was asking her on a date, but he wasn't sure how to do it.

His cheeks heated. Would she say yes? He wasn't sure. Not even after the kiss they'd shared. Especially not after the kiss.

It had been an impulse. He'd wanted to touch her for so long. Maybe he didn't have any lingering feelings. Maybe they'd get it out of their system. Finally. Instead, he was more confused than ever. Meanwhile, she was acting as if it never happened.

He calmed his racing heart. "I'm asking you over to the house for dinner *with* me and Pops. You've been working for hours without a break."

"I wouldn't say no to some of Pops's cooking." Morgan grinned.

He waited while she locked up the gallery. Then she stood next to the *Dorthea Lou* while he closed up the Bait & Tackle Co. Side by side, they took the gravel path to the harbor where his truck was parked. Jesse's strides were long, and he was so caught up in his list of troubles, she was almost running when he slowed down enough to let her catch up.

"Are you sure he'll be okay with it?" she asked. "Pops was never fond of anyone in my family."

Was she having doubts? About him? Or his family? He

hoped not.

"Pops liked your mom," Jesse said. "He liked her a lot. And he's mellowed."

Which wasn't exactly the truth. Pops was many things. Mellow was not one of them.

"I doubt that," Morgan said.

"Truth?" Jesse turned to face her. "He lost his fight after your mom and dad died. He didn't get out of bed for weeks. He was devastated."

"Really?"

Jesse nodded. "Then Mom and Dad bought the condo in Florida and announced they'll be spending Christmas there. He's not happy about it. Me neither. Anyway. He misses your folks. And worries about you."

WHEN JESSE AND Morgan came through the front door, Pops's La-Z-Boy closed with a snap. Two cats and a yellow dog all scattered in different directions as Pops got to his feet. All four, including Jesse's grandpa, looked confused and uncertain as to why their long winter's nap had suddenly come to such a quick and inconvenient ending.

Pops took a moment, and his gaze narrowed on Morgan. "What is she doing here?" he asked. For the first time ever, he didn't seem ready and raring for a fight, even though his eyes were washed-out blue, like Lake Michigan during a snow squall.

"She's here for dinner. Do you have any of the meatloaf left over?" Jesse asked as he opened the fridge and stared inside. He didn't immediately see anything that could be turned into a meal.

"For heaven's sake, we're not going to serve Morgan Adair leftovers. She's a guest in our home. You make the cocktails. I'll start dinner."

"Not gonna lie. She'll eat almost anything," he said. "You don't need to make a fuss."

"Hey," Morgan protested, slapping him on the shoulder. "I'm still company."

"Ask her what she wants to drink." Pops smacked Jesse, forcing him to close the fridge door. "And give her the good stuff."

Jesse filled the wineglass on the counter to the rim like it was a beer pint. Morgan didn't offer any objections. "I hope you like chardonnay," Jesse said.

She nodded and picked up the glass, without pausing her comfortable chat with Pops.

Within the hour there were a half-dozen delicious scents coming from the kitchen—fresh whitefish, tarragon, leeks, and mustard. Pops was pulling out all the stops. Jesse's mouth watered in anticipation of all his favorite comfort foods.

"I'm grateful for the help you've given Jesse," Pops said.

"Jesse's very talented," Morgan said. "He should have a

gallery of his own. Plus, since I've been back in Fish Village, I've been working on solving a mystery."

"What mystery, girl detective?" Jesse teased.

"Do you remember the tree that always appeared on Christmas Eve? Turns out Pete Blomquist started the tradition and his family carried it on for the next forty years. In the fifties and sixties, Fermin Wiggs took over the tree duties to comfort his homesick wife. Then one of Skip's relatives did it as a memorial for his wife. The Kimuras took over in 1998 when they moved here from San Francisco. But after that, the trail goes cold."

"And you call yourself a detective," Jesse said.

Morgan raised an eyebrow, but didn't take the bait. Instead, she turned to Pops. "What do you know about the floating Christmas tree that you're not telling?"

He looked at Jesse, then back at Morgan. "Nothing. That's my story and I'm sticking to it." Pops said with a twinkle in his eye.

Jesse couldn't remember when he'd been so content. The playful banter between the two people he cared about most in the world warmed him right down to his toes.

But Morgan was relentless. "Spill your secrets, Pops," she demanded.

"Dinner's almost ready," Pops changed the subject and shooed Jesse and Morgan out of the kitchen. "Why don't you two set the table? Use the good china."

Morgan flashed a cheeky grin. "Pops is treating me like

company."

"I told you that he'd be glad to see you."

Jesse laid the silverware on the placemats, while Morgan followed behind him, rearranging and reorganizing everything he did. More than once, their fingers intertwined. Jesse pulled her close, holding her close while checking over his shoulder to make sure Pops wouldn't catch them in an embrace. She pushed him away just as Pops came out of the kitchen with the first of many platters of food.

Morgan and Jesse settled as the table while Pops served the meal family-style. Morgan learned quickly she had to eat fast to keep up with Jesse and his grandfather.

"This is delicious," Morgan said with her mouth full. She licked her lips. Jesse had to turn away to keep from staring too long.

"I was glad to hear you kids put Hillcrest House on the market," Pops said. "I don't like the idea of you clattering around in that old house all by yourself."

"I know it's a good thing," Morgan said. "But I don't know what I going to do when it sells."

Jesse's cellphone rang, interrupted any further discussion. "Excuse me," he said. "I've got to grab this."

He stood in the hallway, trying to comprehend what the guy on the phone was saying, all while eavesdropping on Morgan's conversation with Pops. It was futile.

"Hey, I'm sorry to cancel on you at the last minute," the guy on the phone said. "I need to call off tomorrow." Well, that grabbed him back to reality. What was he going to do now?

When he returned to the table, Morgan read him like a book. "What's going on?" she asked.

"The guy who was going to help me on the boat tomorrow can't make it. It's the last run of the season." He shook his head. "Without another guy . . . I can't do it alone. There's no reason to take Dot out."

"I'll go," Morgan volunteered.

Pops was silent. Jesse was torn. He wanted to spend the day with her, but he wasn't so sure it was a good idea. He shook his head. "I don't know."

"Dad always said I was his best mate." she grinned.

"Doubt she'll take no for an answer," Pops said. His approval was all the encouragement Jesse needed.

The muscles in Jesse's neck and shoulders relaxed as he nodded. "You're right. I've lost this battle before. When will I ever learn?"

Morgan cleared the table and washed the dishes after dinner. She moved toward the front door. "I guess I should take off," she said with a wink. Jesse's heart sunk. He wasn't ready for her to leave.

Pops reached for her hand. His hands practically swallowed hers. "Thanks for coming to dinner."

"It was great to see you again." She was so sweet with the old man, covering his hand with her own. "I'm sorry it's been so long. We'll have to do this again sometime soon."

"I'd like that." Pops grinned.

Jesse guided her out the door, shouting over his shoulder, "I'll be right back," as he stepped out onto the porch with Morgan. As soon as they were alone, he reached out and stroked her dark hair. Silky to the touch. As perfect as ever. He separated the strands.

Morgan checked over her shoulder. "Stop it. Pops is just inside."

"You honestly think he doesn't know?" He shook his head. "The only person who doesn't suspect you and I were ever romantically involved is you."

Morgan shushed him and pulled his hand away from her hair. He smiled in spite of himself. She was stubborn, and he didn't want to argue.

"I'll walk you home," he said.

She put her hand on his and stopped him. Instinctively, he curled his fingers around hers. She didn't pull away. They were both content to stand close together in the darkness, holding onto each other's hands.

"What time do I need to be in the harbor?" she asked.

"Four-thirty?"

She winced. "Then I better get going."

Jesse nodded. Then she smiled up at him. Holding nothing back. Before she turned to go, Jesse was nearly knocked to his knees. He'd met his match.

Chapter Fifteen

December 22

THREE HOURS BEFORE sunrise, Morgan was shaking with cold, clinging to the door handle in Jeff's truck. The harbor was pitch black, and an arctic blast off Lake Michigan nearly shattered her resolve to help Jesse as she jumped down out of the cab.

"Thanks for the ride," she said, gathering up the extra warm clothes off the passenger seat she'd brought with her to carry out onto the tug. Another blast of cold air almost cut her in two. Five more minutes out in the elements, and her teeth were going to start chattering. How did her dad do this every day?

"You sure you guys will be all right?" Jeff leaned across the steering wheel to catch her eye. "How long has it been since you've been out?"

"More than a few years." Morgan laughed, but she quickly dismissed his concern. "It'll be fine."

"It's not like flying a plane," Jeff said.

"I'm an Adair. Fishing is our first language. I've got this." She faked a confident smile as she waved goodbye. In truth, she wasn't so sure. Watching Jeff circle the parking lot, she second- and third-guessed her decision.

A lake-effect snow shower had left its mark overnight, leaving Christmas Tree Cove looking as if it were dusted with powdered sugar. The ice crunched beneath her feet as she found her way across the gravel path down to Fish Village.

Jesse was in the pilothouse of the *Dorthea Lou*, with the engines idling in the water, when she stepped out onto the docks. Morgan nodded her greeting, and Jesse nodded back. Not exactly an overwhelming public display of affection. Especially after the kiss they'd shared. The one that made her heart flutter and her cheeks burn with heat. A strange phenomenon when the weather for the past few days had been like a direct blast from the Arctic Circle.

No talking.

It was an unwritten rule among the fishermen who went out before dawn. It was too early for conversation. If they had anything to say, it could wait until the sun was up over the horizon and the tug was out in the waves.

Morgan glanced at Jesse and nearly burst out laughing. "You're really wearing a cashmere sweater out on the boat?"

"It'll keep me warm," Jesse said. "And I've got an old sweatshirt to put over it."

"I doubt that'll protect it from the fish smell." She wrinkled up her nose. "Where did you get the braces?"

"Pops," he said. "There's another pair hanging behind

the door you can use." He nodded toward the nearby fish shanty.

Morgan pushed open the door to the shanty. Since the Taylors had taken over her family's fishing business, this tiny shanty wasn't used very often. She wasn't sure she'd ever been inside. It was like a time capsule from the 1940s.

Morgan pulled on the fisherman's bib and braces, hoping to postpone getting wet for as long as possible, and then returned to the dock near the *Dorthea Lou.*

"You all set?" Jesse asked.

"Yep." She gave a big thumbs-up.

Jesse returned to the pilothouse to throttle up and steer away from the docks. Morgan stood on the dock to pull the lines. She swung up onto the deck of the tug in one easy motion while it was underway, as if she'd been doing it all her life. She and Jesse were both operating from lessons they had learned when they were kids. Still, it had been a long time since she had been out pulling nets. Morgan was still worried the years had eroded her skills and could get them into serious trouble. This gig wasn't for amateurs.

Waving to get Jesse's attention, she pointed at the sun rising over Christmas Tree Cove, lighting up the pointed pencil tops of the pine trees on Sugar Hill, and turning the water bright blue. Once the tug was beyond the break wall, the waves became choppy. White foam rose on the edge of the boat as Jesse turned into the wind, instinctively finding his way to the Taylors' semi-secret fishing location. The tug pounded into the waves with spray spitting across the bow. Morgan stood in the bow of the boat, letting water splash on her face.

She was abundantly happy as Jesse turned the tug to the north. She'd done this so many times, but this was the first time she'd ever been out without her dad. Her throat tightened.

Morgan stumbled into the pilothouse, sitting down on the bench behind Jesse. The tiny pilothouse reeked of kerosene from the heater he had started to create the illusion of warmth.

He nodded toward a lunchbox tucked below the bench. When she opened it, she made a small sound in the back of her throat. Wrapped in wax paper and cut on the diagonal were breakfast sandwiches, the same kind her mom used to make them when they were in high school. She had forgotten all about them, but Jesse remembered. She was so touched by his kindness, she wanted to wrap herself around him in an unending hug, but she didn't dare.

Morgan poured two cups of coffee out of a thermos. She handed one cup to Jesse. It wasn't anything fancy. Not like the stuff they served at the Bait & Tackle Co. She didn't think he'd complain.

Morgan sat on the cover of the forward hold to eat her breakfast sandwich, turning out of the wind to face the aft of the boat. She watched the sun rise over the cove, until they were out past the lighthouse.

Long, golden rays of light made the cresting waves sparkle as if they were aquamarine crystals. She smiled despite the crisp, cold air. It was a magical winter's day.

When she was a kid, the last fishing trip of the season was always planned for the first day of her Christmas break. She'd spend the day out on the water helping her dad. It was the same for Jesse. At the end of the day, everyone who worked in Fish Village went out for dinner. She and Jesse had a separate table from the adults, who celebrated the end of the season with animated big fish stories, some more truthful than others. She'd been perfectly content sitting close to Jesse while listening to her dad's booming laughter at the next table.

Caught up in memories, she didn't stir again until they arrived at their designated fishing location for the day. Morgan and Jesse worked together in a series of choreographed movements they'd learned when they were kids. It had been a long time since either of them had been out on the water, but their steps were instinctive.

Pulling a pair of aviator sunglasses out of her pocket, she pushed them up her nose. They worked in silence. It wasn't long before the holds were full, and Jesse pulled the lines and turned the boat toward home. Morgan sat on the bench behind him in the pilothouse.

"You okay?" he asked, shouting over the sound of the engines.

Morgan nodded. She was lying. Her stomach was feeling

a little squirrelly. The kerosene from the heater. The diesel fuel. The fish. All were strong aromas that clung to everything, and together, they were a lethal, one-two punch.

The holds were filled with ice and the catch of the day. The little tug wasn't skimming over the top of the waves. It was chugging through the deep-blue water, slamming down into waves. It was a lurching, uncomfortable roller-coaster ride.

She left the pilothouse and stood at the side of the boat, letting the water spray across her face while the waves pounded the tug.

"Hey," Jesse shouted.

"Hey what?"

"I'm checking to see if you're alright," Jesse said. "We're gonna have a pretty bumpy ride for the rest of the trip."

She let go of a big breath, hoping it would help settle her stomach. But it didn't. Not even a little. The odds that she was going to be sick were getting higher with each passing minute, but she didn't want Jesse to know. She didn't want to look weak. Not here. Not today. Not in front of him. "I'm fine," she muttered.

"I've been feeling green around the gills too."

She searched his face. "You look"—Handsome. Hotter, really, than ever. How that was possible, she had no clue—"really good. As usual."

He shook his head. "We're running so deep with the catch onboard and a steady chop from the west. We're getting tossed pretty good. It's a deadly combination."

She rested her forehead against her arm. All of her energy was going toward keeping from getting sick. "I'm afraid I'm going to be sick."

"Your mind is just playing tricks on you. It's a sensory mismatch between what your eyes are seeing and what your inner ear is feeling," he said. "Look at the horizon line. Sometimes that helps."

She took a deep breath and looked at the shoreline, hoping to get her bearings. But with a storm brewing in the distance the water and the sky had blended together along the horizon making it impossible for her to up from down and making her woozy. She pressed her tongue against the roof of her mouth.

"It's been a rougher ride out here than I expected. I usually only get motion sickness on a plane when my fate is out of my control." Behind his sunglasses, she couldn't see his eyes to tell if he was being honest or sarcastic. "Are you going to be sick?"

Morgan shook her head. It was wishful thinking. "I hope not."

"Okay. I'll let you be." He went back inside the pilothouse. She was relieved.

Strands of hair danced in front of her face. She was going to be sick. The bile was rising up in her throat. No turning back. All she could do was find a place where it would create the least amount of mess. She forced herself to take three wobbly steps. Clawing at her face to move the clumps of hair away from her mouth, she leaned over the side of the tug a moment before she lost her entire breakfast.

Jesse put a warm hand on her back. He tamed her hair with the other.

"Jesse, please don't."

He let go and stepped back. "Please don't what?"

"I don't want you to see me like this," she choked out between spasms.

"Are you kidding?" Jesse shouted. "This is nothing. I've seen you in way worse shape than this."

"No, you haven't," she spat back. "No one has seen me like this."

"What?" He guffawed. "Who held your hair back the night you attempted to drink three bottles of strawberry wine on Senior Dare Night?"

"Jesse. I can't. Not right now. I'm going to be sick again." And then she was. Choking and gasping, she emptied her stomach until she was down to dry heaves.

She leaned back on her knees, taking big, gulping breaths of the cold, clean air. Jesse handed her a towel to wipe her face.

"You feeling any better?" he asked.

She nodded. "I've lost my sea legs." She'd always been strong and capable. It was her flex, but her swagger had disappeared. "I'm sorry. I didn't want to be a hindrance to you out here."

"You're fine. This is not a problem," he said. "My real problem is that I misplaced my code book for deciphering Morgan Adair six years ago. And I sure as hell didn't know I'd ever need it again."

Morgan closed and opened her eyes dramatically. "I'm not that difficult."

"The hell you aren't," he snapped. "The only emotion that coaxes you out of hiding any more is anger. That's the only reason you came back to Fish Village. I made you angry enough to do it."

"I was scared," she said.

"Of what?"

"All the ghosts in Fish Village."

"It's not the dead that scare you, Morgan. It's the living."

Morgan pressed her lips together. "I don't want to have this conversation."

"Let me assure you, the last thing I want to do with you right now is talk," he said. "Even though we haven't had a real conversation in six years."

The words burst out of her. "You went to Chicago without me."

"You ghosted me," he said. "Without a single word of explanation."

She recoiled a little, not knowing whether she should ask for his forgiveness or defend her actions. "I had to make sure my brother and sisters were okay, and I didn't want to argue with you about it."

He shook his head. "You could've told me anything and I would've believed you. But I couldn't stand your silence."

The wind cutting across the waves was bone chilling. She closed her eyes. Morgan sagged against him, overheated from being sick. The skin on the back of her neck prickled. She rubbed her hand across her mouth, wishing she had something to rinse out the bad taste. "I need to swish, but I left my water bottle in the bridge."

"Here. Take mine." Jesse pulled one out of the pocket of his coat and handed it to her. She took a swig.

"I'm scared, Jesse," she whispered. "What am I going to do?"

Chapter Sixteen

S HE CURLED INTO his arms and tucked her head under his chin. Then Morgan opened her eyes and nailed him with a look. Even in her queasy state, her green eyes bewitched him, leaving him with mixed emotions.

I'm scared, Jesse.

He'd waited so long for her to share her emotions with him. He wasn't completely sure this was happening. His coat was unzipped. She attempted to snuggle into his puffer jacket. He resisted a little, then opened one side to let her warm her limbs. She snuggled closer.

Against his better judgment, he hugged her tighter. He'd wanted to be with her for so long, but he was still wary. What did she want?

"That's not true, Morgan. You're not scared. You've never been afraid of anything."

"Maybe when I was younger. But after barely holding on for six years, my life is changing. It's completely out of control. And it's coming at me so fast I'm losing touch with the things that really matter."

"Like what?"

"Things that remind me of my parents."

When was the last time she'd confided in him? It had to be at least six years ago on Christmas Eve. His mind was spinning.

"After six years of being in control and avoiding human interaction, I'm having so many emotions. Sometimes one kind of blends with another, and I have a hard time recognizing what I'm really feeling." She took another sip of water.

"We all get that way from time to time." Jesse wasn't sure what his expectation has been for this fishing trip, but having Morgan expose her bare-naked emotions wasn't in the plans. He was on shaky ground.

He swallowed hard. Seeing her so open and vulnerable left him with so many questions, he wasn't sure where to start. If he asked, would she tell him the truth? Or would she run away and hide again? He was uncertain.

"You don't have to start making changes all at once. Take it bit by bit."

"I can't go on the way I've been. I've been gripping so hard for too long. I'm afraid I can't let go long enough to go after what I really want."

"What do you really want?"

She looked up at him. "That's a good question."

"Taking a first step is an act of faith, much like your beloved floating Christmas tree."

She shook her head. "It was my mom who believed in

that tree. Eli believed it was Santa who put the tree out to let all the kids in Christmas Tree Cove know he'd delivered all the presents. I thought it was a place to make Christmas wishes handled by magical elves sent by Santa, but Mom knew the truth all along. It was always about true love."

"Every kid who grew up in Christmas Tree Cove believed it was some kind of magic. It's probably why the tradition was continued for so long." Jesse shifted his position. A smile stretched the corners of his mouth. His eyes remained on the same hazy spot on the horizon. "Nothing's holding you back now, Morgan. Take a leap of faith and see where you land. And if you make a mistake, you can always have a do-over."

She shook her head. "I'm fairly certain I've used up all my do-overs."

"No way. I've already logged a couple thousand do-overs in the last six years. No one has a crystal ball. No one can see into the future. My mom and dad bought a condo in Florida. They want to become snowbirds, and Pops will need more care in the winter."

"Can you take care of him?"

"Not when I'm working in New York," he said. "I really need the gallery to be a success."

Morgan nodded. "What about your sister? Can you count on her?"

Jesse grinned. "We'll see. She's still in school and focused on classes."

Morgan nodded. "I get it."

He'd wished for this moment with her. Right here. Right now. All was right in his world. *To work things out. To talk to you. To understand each other. To make sure we're okay. That's what I want. Nothing more.*

"So your whole world is changing too?"

He grinned broadly. "Pretty much."

Laughing and smiling, their faces inches away from each other, it was almost as if nothing had ever kept them apart. Jesse closed his eyes. "I want you to be happy. I want you to be loved. I want you to live a long and happy life."

"Me too. I want all those things for you," she said. "Are you happy?"

"I've moved forward," he said. "My heart hasn't. Not yet."

"Jesse . . ." she said, but he stopped her with a heated look.

"It doesn't have anything to do with you. And it does. It has everything to do with you. No one has ever measured up to you. No one has ever made me as happy. No one has ever understood me. No one has ever infuriated me as much as you do. But I don't want us to go six years without speaking again. I want you to be a part of my life."

Morgan bit her lip, hesitating. "I'm still not sure we're heading in the same direction."

"The world is wide and amazing. But this is the corner of the world I want to live in. It's my choice. And I've made it."

Looking out over Lake Michigan, Jesse took a moment to gather his thoughts. "I came back, but not until I was grown up enough to admit Christmas Tree Cove is the only place I can be me. I can breathe. I can be myself. I fit in. It's perfect. For me. What are you going to choose?"

Morgan shook her head. "I don't know."

They were both silent for a moment. He was feeling a bit flustered. Had he said too much? She wouldn't look him in the eyes. She smiled, but it was a bit forced. "I guess we can't fool around anymore."

"Nope. You feeling any better?"

She brushed her hair off her face. "I think I'm going to make it."

"Then we should get rolling. We need to beat this storm to shore." Jesse untangled himself from Morgan and went back to the helm.

The dark wall of clouds churning behind them made him nervous. He didn't mind letting the winds in front of the storm push them back into the harbor, but he didn't want to be caught in the middle of it.

Jesse set a course back to the harbor. Neither one of them spoke for the rest of the trip. Jesse was still digesting their conversation while Morgan concentrated all of her energy on maintaining visual contact with the lighthouse. Her face was pale and drawn. He had no doubt she was still a little queasy.

When they got back to Fish Village, they went about

their separate tasks with the same quiet camaraderie. Morgan efficiently wrapped the lines on the dock, while Jesse ducked into his family's fishing shanty and prepared to unload the fresh catch from the holds.

"You can take off. I've got it from here."

But Morgan had never followed directions well. Instead she tagged along behind him into the shanty. Watching all of his movements in silence. Her close-up observations made him nervous, but he was very confident in his knife skills as he methodically prepped the fish to be smoked, using quick, firm cuts.

"You going to smoke tomorrow?"

Jesse nodded. "Yep. First thing."

"You'll need to have all the fish cleaned tonight," she said.

It wasn't a question. It was a statement.

He nodded. "I already told you. I can handle it."

She shook her head. "I'm not leaving here until my job is done."

She shrugged out of her jacket and pulled on a rubber apron. Then she joined him at the table, standing by his side she started to fillet fish. When she wasn't looking, he checked her work. She went slowly at first, but made the precise cuts necessary, so none of the flesh was wasted.

"How's this?" Morgan held up her work for Jesse's review.

He looked it over. "Not bad."

She grinned and got back to work. Jesse searched his mind for something to say.

Words. Words would be good here.

A mindless conversation didn't seem right. Not after they'd been able to speak honestly and openly about their feelings on the boat. They'd cleared the air. They'd caught up. Now they had both gone back to their separate corners and all communication had stopped.

A knot of dread formed in his stomach. Maybe he'd said too much out on the boat. When it was just the two of them. He'd backed her into a corner and put all the blame on her.

He glanced down at her. Morgan looked up at him through her lashes, but avoided any eye contact. Maybe working in silence was for the best.

He found a beer in the fridge under the worktable. He offered it to her first. She took a long pull and handed it back to him. He did the same and then set the bottle on the table between them. They took turns taking sips.

He turned on an ancient transistor radio that had been set on the two-by-four in the exposed walls sometime in the seventies. It could only tune in one station, an AM radio station from Wisconsin playing tinny Christmas music.

They'd been out on the boat since hours before the sunrise. And now, two hours after sunset, they were still working. The day wasn't done until the catch was cleaned and packed on fresh ice in the cooler.

Morgan was rinsing her hands off in the sink when Jesse

dropped his jacket over her shoulders. He'd noticed the temperature in the shanty had dropped sharply. "Thank you," she said.

"There's a hand warmer in one pocket," Jesse whispered. "A butterscotch in the other. You can have both."

She pulled his coat closer. Their fingers momentarily touched, and they both pulled away as if they'd been burned by a flame. She turned off the taps and stepped back to dry her hands on towel when her stomach grumbled.

Jesse laughed. "You must be feeling better."

"I'm actually starving."

"It's whitefish night at The Sip. Grilled and blackened or batter-dipped and fried."

"That sounds so good."

Just then Grace stuck her head in the door. "The light was on," she said with an easy smile. "Thought I'd stop by. I didn't know you'd both be here."

"We were talking about getting whitefish at The Sip," Jesse said, washing his hands in the sink.

"I'm in," Grace grinned. "This'll be fun."

By the time he'd dried off his hands, Morgan's eyes had clouded. She was distracted.

"Listen, I'm going to bow out," Morgan said. "I forgot that I'm flying in the morning. And I lost my breakfast, lunch, and dinner out on the boat today. I should really go home and take it easy."

"Are you sure?" Jesse asked.

She nodded. "Absolutely. You guys go. Have fun."

He wasn't sure how to say goodbye. He wanted to envelop her in a hug, but the way she was standing didn't invite any kind of physical contact. "Thank you for your help. I really appreciate it."

Morgan smiled. "It was my pleasure. Thank you for the rescue."

She ducked out the door and was gone in a heartbeat. Jesse turned off the light and followed Grace out the door.

Something made him glance over his shoulder. Morgan hadn't gone straight home. She was standing on the end of the dock in Fish Village. The snow falling softly in the moonlight. He wanted to capture it on camera.

"Go ahead and get a table," he said. "I'll catch up."

Grace looked at Morgan, a knowing smile on her face before she wandered down the dock.

Jesse grabbed his camera from a hook on the wall in the fishing shanty. He quietly approached Morgan.

Her cellphone rang. He stopped.

Morgan answered without looking at the caller ID. "Hey, Skip. What's up?" she said. "Yeah. I really appreciate your offer . . ."

She turned her head, and the wind carried the rest of her words in the other direction. He didn't want to intrude on her privacy.

Now is not the time.

He turned around and walked away.

Chapter Seventeen

December 23

T HE SKY WAS turning pink along the horizon when Morgan pulled up and parked her truck in front of Northwoods Aviation. Six inches of snow had fallen over-night, but the snowplows had been out early. The roads to the airport were clear and dry.

She blew out a long, frosty plume of air, hoping to calm her racing heart threatening to beat its way out of her chest. She had never been nervous before a flight, but today was different.

Are you crazy? Why did you agree to this?

She took a deep breath to calm her nerves.

You got this? Sure. I do.

She grinned and got out of the truck. She hated the way she looked when she was dressed as a pilot. Wearing a uniform that had been designed for a man didn't work on her curvy body, but she hoped no one would notice. She took another shaky breath to help her gather up her courage to take flight in a way she never had before.

Morgan's mind kept drifting back to Jesse.

When she blinked, he was standing right in front of her, his hand outstretched with a peppermint candy. Morgan shook her head. She needed to stay focused, or else he would appear again. Smiling. Tempting her. Reminding her of feelings she'd tried so hard to forget. How she'd broken his heart. And her own.

Morgan forced herself to focus. She didn't have time for feelings. Not this morning. She didn't have time to unpack and sort through her feelings for Jesse.

Concentrate.

She stopped at the bottom of the stairs leading up to the executive jet. She grinned. Flying this jet would keep her mind occupied. It was the distraction she so desperately needed.

Morgan had declined Skip's invitation to fly as a part of the crew on the executive jet she'd admired so many times before. She wasn't sure why she'd said yes this time, but she'd decided it was because the time she'd been spending with Jesse was giving her a renewed feeling of confidence.

She jogged up the steps and ducked in throught the exit door. A tall pilot greeted her immediately. "You must be Morgan Adair," he said. "I'm Jim Shelton, and I'll be your captain today."

He introduced her to the other pilot, who was settling into one of the roomy leather seats in the main cabin.

"We're flying an empty leg to Chicago Midway to pick up a passenger," the captain said. "We've got a full flight crew, but our first officer is going to ride in the back so you can sit with me in the flight deck on the left-hand side in the first officer's seat."

Morgan nodded and followed the captain, slipping into the tight confines of the cockpit. She settled into the first officer's seat, marveling at all the computer displays, dials and read-outs on the panels in the confined space. She was familiar with most, but not all.

"Definitely a Lambo," she muttered under her breath.

Jim slid into the right-side seat. "Aren't you forgetting something?" he asked.

"Beg your pardon?"

"If you're going to sit in that seat," the captain said, "it's your job to check out the airworthiness of the aircraft."

Check out this jet? Don't mind if I do.

"If you have any questions, tell the guy riding in the back to give you a hand."

The first officer was very chatty as he gave her a tour outside of the jet. She responded to all of his questions with a big smile. She could hardly wait to fly.

Sliding back into her seat in the flight deck, she pulled on her headset. The captain finished his preflight check and asked permission from the tower to taxi out to the runway, where they waited for their final clearance.

"You ready for this?" the captain asked. Morgan gave him a thumbs-up.

The pilot adjusted the throttle. The plane accelerated on

the runway and quickly reached speed. The nose of the plane lifted and began to climb.

He handled the controls with deft precision. Now and then he included Morgan in his instructions through the headset. "Okay. I'm going to reduce thrust to climb power, and accelerate the aircraft toward 250 knots, retracting flaps and slats."

A few minutes later they broke through the clouds, and the sun came in through the windows, lighting up the flight deck. Morgan checked the altimeter. They were at three thousand feet.

"How do you feel?" he asked.

She beamed brightly. "Most days I don't fly above a ceiling of five hundred feet. This is a dream come true."

He smiled. "I was worried you were going to be a much tougher customer."

Morgan took a cockpit selfie. Her fingers hovered over her phone, deciding whether or not to send it to Jesse. Maybe she should wait and tell him in person after the grand opening party. Then she'd be able to see his face. Suddenly, she had so many reasons to celebrate this Christmas.

The forty-five-minute flight to Chicago went by in a split second. Morgan was still adjusting to the controls in the unfamiliar cockpit when the captain contacted the tower at Midway Airport to request clearance to land.

To no one's surprise, Chicago air traffic was a mess. They were put in a holding pattern to await further instructions. They were late by the time the tower finally cleared them. But the captain finessed the executive jet into the gentlest touchdown bump and roll Morgan had ever seen.

She couldn't stop smiling. Even after it took twenty minutes to taxi to a small group of hangers where a red carpet had been rolled out on the tarmac.

"Big shout-out to the guys from the FBO for giving us the red-carpet treatment," Jim said before removing his headset. He stayed seated, but Morgan got up and went back into the cabin. The first officer was already opening the aircraft door. The captain was so accurate with his parking, the steps fell directly onto the red carpet.

At the bottom of the stairs, the client was waiting next to a small rolling suitcase.

Morgan looked down into the face of her unflappable, I-don't-need-anything-sugarcoated-for-me sister, Dacey, and immediately burst into tears.

Running down the steps, she threw her arms around her. "You're the client we're picking up?"

"You're my pilot?" Dacey asked.

"Maybe," she said. "I'm thinking about learning to fly jets."

"Thinking about it?" Dacey asked. "Just say yes."

Morgan nodded.

"My boss gave me this empty leg flight for Christmas," Dacey said. "I'll still have to work from Christmas Tree Cove over the holidays. But I'll be with you guys."

Morgan grinned. "You're the best handmade Christmas present ever."

"Remind Kayla of that when you see her."

The flight back to Traverse City was almost as much fun and the outbound flight had been. Skip picked up Morgan and Dacey at the Traverse City airport and took them home, making a picture-perfect landing in the harbor at exactly 3:13 p.m.

"Welcome to Christmas Tree Cove," he said, pulling alongside the dock to deplane.

"Are you coming to the grand opening tonight?" Morgan asked.

"Wouldn't miss it." Skip grinned. "I heard the flight to Chicago went well."

"Better than I ever expected."

"I'm glad to hear it. We'll have to talk after the holidays."

"You bet," Morgan said.

Eli was waiting for them next to his car in the harbor parking lot. He'd driven up from Ann Arbor, bringing beer to be served at the gallery's grand opening night. He loaded Dacey and her suitcase in the car to take her off to Hillcrest House.

Morgan waved goodbye, then took the path to Fish Village.

Every inch of the gallery had been decorated with fairy lights. The big front window display was filled with two oversized photographs Jesse had taken of the floating Christmas tree over the years. They were hanging next to a sepia-toned poster of the first tree on Christmas Tree Cove, on loan from the museum.

By the time the two guys Eli had hired to run the bar arrived, Morgan was in a celebratory mood. While they were setting up the bar service, the first trays of charcuterie arrived from the Bait & Tackle Co. Morgan slipped into the back storeroom to change into her green party dress, and when she returned to the gallery, she was a whirling ball of party prep.

Forty-five minutes later, the gallery was crowded. There were so many people in attendance at the party she hadn't been in touch with in such a long time. Her third-grade teacher. The guy who'd changed her tire by the side of the road two years ago. The woman who worked with her behind the counter at Bait & Tackle Co. one summer when she was in high school. They'd all were there to celebrate the gallery's grand opening.

At some point, Jesse appeared, dressed all in black—a leather jacket over a turtleneck. He made her heart skip a beat. He'd never looked so handsome.

Jesse was the man of the hour. Everyone wanted to talk to him. He was constantly surrounded by admirers who wanted him to sign their recently purchased photograph.

Morgan tried once or twice to catch his gaze, but his eyes were hidden behind the dark wing of his hair. When he finally focused all of his attention on her, he flashed a quick smile. It was as if a bottle rocket were in the pit of her stomach, lighted and sparkling in anticipation of something more in the very near future.

Morgan stood back and admired Jesse from afar. His wide smile. His deep laugh.

You're in love with him.

Morgan ignored the little voice in her head and instead worked her way to the back of the crowded gallery, where she hung out in the shadows as the party unfolded before her eyes.

Minutes later, the crowd parted, and Jesse appeared. He pressed into the space next to her in the shadows. The brush of his fingertips along the bare skin of her forearm sent tingles down her spine.

She reached for him. Their fingers tangled and entwined. Hiding in plain sight was a trick they'd learned when they were in high school. He'd tug her hand, and then they'd quietly sneak away. To a quiet place. Their place. Where they could talk and touch without anyone else noticing. Mostly, she talked and he listened. She was always making plans. Big plans. And Jesse encouraged her. Supported her.

She couldn't remember the speficifs of any of their conversations, but she could remember Jesse's kisses. They were always sweet and delicious. Almost as warm and comforting as being wrapped in his arms.

Jesse disentangled his fingers from hers, bringing Morgan

back from her memories.

"I'll be right back," he said. "Hold my place."

She nodded. All her attention was focused on him as he moved through the crowded space.

"Hey, do you want something to drink?" Eli asked, leaning over her shoulder.

Pivoting on her heel, she turned into a circle that included her brother and both of her sisters. "No. I want to keep my hands free," she said. "Just in case."

Morgan smiled when Jesse joined the group. A dark scowl on his face. His legs planted wide and his arms crossed over his chest. Something was bothering him. Glancing around the room, she searched in vain for the source of his irritation.

"Jesse," Kayla said, "this is an amazing turnout for the gallery opening. Can you believe how many people are here? You must be pleased."

"This is all your sister's doing. I didn't lift a finger." He flashed a quick smile in her direction and Morgan's anxiety melted away.

"Have you heard the big news of the day?" Eli asked. "Our Morgan-a is going to go to flight school in Chicago."

Morgan looked up in time to catch Jesse's startled reaction.

"Let's not get ahead of ourselves. Nothing is for certain yet." Morgan protested.

"That is big," Jesse said in a sober tone, his face unreadable. "I had no idea you were making plans to leave Christmas Tree Cove."

"It's not like that." Morgan shook her head. "I don't have an specific plans. Skip made arrangements for me to fly an executive jet with a crew out of Chicago this morning." She forced a smile, hoping Jesse would smile back, but he wouldn't make eye contact with her.

Jesse looked over her head to the far side of the crowded gallery. "Well. You've had a very busy day," he said. "Will you excuse me? I see some clients I need to tend to."

"Yes. Of course. It's your night," she said.

Jesse nodded and disappeared into the crowd.

MORGAN TOOK A lap around the party. She didn't bump into Jesse, but she was happy every photograph in the gallery had a round dot next to the title under the display. They'd sold everything. Some people took the photographs off the wall and carried them home under their arm. Others were happy to wait for their orders to be filled after Christmas.

She was wrapping a photograph in brown paper when a movement near the door drew her attention. She instinctively searched for Jesse's tall form in the crowd.

Once. Twice. Three times.

She glanced over her shoulder. Realization slowly dawned on her.

He was gone.

He'd slipped away the same way he had when they were kids. An unspoken promise sent fingers of electricity through her body as she anticipated the possibilities of being alone with Jesse.

She took a moment to check on her family. Kayla and Jeff were focused on the photographs. Eli was pouring tasting flights. Dacey had found Grace, and they were now giggling in the corner.

No one was paying attention to her. Everyone was too busy enjoying themselves.

Morgan ttook a deep breath to stay calm and keep her movements from drawing unwanted attention as she slipped out the front door of the gallery.

A vintage Chris-Craft wooden boat decorated with brightly colored lights steered up the river in Fish Village. The big V-8 engine rumbled as its occupants shouted Christmas greetings to everyone standing out on the dock.

Morgan waved back. "Merry Christmas!"

She stepped off the dock onto the gravel path next to the gallery. Anticipation buzzed in the pit of her stomach. She held her breath until she was certain of the crunch of gravel under her feet. Then she broke into a sprint toward the bench Jesse had kept intact when he'd rebuilt Obermeyer's shanty.

She couldn't move fast enough. The path between the shanties was pitch black, but she had done this so many when she was younger, she could find her way by muscle memory alone.

He was waiting for her, long and lean, standing in the darkness, his hands in his pockets, his profile lit by the moonlight. His masculine beauty almost took her breath away.

"Jesse?" she whispered.

He turned around. The dark scowl on his face had returned. It was the last thing she expected to see.

Chapter Eighteen

"Jesse?"

Morgan's dark hair blew back over her shoulders and he needed a moment to catch his breath. She was mesmerizing . . . and completely infuriating.

He'd called Matt Wendell and turned down the job in New York City. Decision made, he'd hurried back to Christmas Tree Cove, looking forward to the party and seeing Morgan again. Together, they'd make plans for their future. Instead, every person he talked to at the party mentioned how Morgan Adair had flown a jet and was making plans to go to the pilot training program in Chicago. He couldn't look directly at her, knowing she was a heartbreaker in a green party dress.

"What's going on?" she asked, looking up at his face expectantly. "You aren't happy."

"I'm good," he said. Even though it wasn't true.

She smiled and moved closer. He took a step back and sat down on the bench. When he'd slipped outside, he'd hoped for a few minutes alone to let his anger cool off.

"I don't get it. Are you angry?" she asked. "With me?"

She sat down on the bench next to him, quickly closing the space between them. "The grand opening is a huge success. We couldn't fit one more person inside the gallery."

He took off his glasses and cleaned them with a cloth from his pocket. When he put them back on his face, he raked his fingers through his hair. "Are you kidding? There's still a line of people waiting on the dock to get in."

"We sold every one of the 'On Christmas Tree Cove' posters. Grace is so pleased. Do you know how much money we've raised for the museum foundation?"

He shook his head. "I don't know how you pulled it off in such a short period of time."

"I had a lot of help." Her voice bubbled with confidence. "You know what it's like in Fish Village. As soon as someone finds out you're planning something, they're always willing to lend a hand or help out." She smiled. "I'd forgotten."

He nodded. "It's not always easy to ask for help."

"No. I should've done it sooner." She leaned back against him in search of body heat, and he instinctively pulled away. He was so torn between wanting her, wanting to be closer to her, and indulging his anger.

She turned to face him with her arms crossed over her chest. "What is going on?"

"Why didn't you tell me?" The words burst from him as if he'd been holding them in for years, not minutes. His eyes narrowed as he glared at her.

"Wait. You're really mad? At me?" She asked in genuine

surprise. "What exactly was I supposed to tell you?"

"What did you do this morning?" Jesse raised an eyebrow.

"Are you kidding? That's what you're mad about? Yes. I took the morning off, but I was here until almost midnight last night getting ready for tonight."

"You don't have to account for your time. What I'm asking is why you didn't tell me you flew a jet this morning? That you're going into the pilot training. And moving to Chicago."

She threw up her arms. "I haven't made any decisions about my future."

"That's not what I heard."

"You're listening to what someone else says instead of me? After you warned me about listening to the gossip in Fish Village?" she fired back.

"I'm pretty sure there's a lot more truth in what I heard than any tall tales that ever went around about me and Grace. We were whispered about because we were the only two single people under forty in Fish Village. But you didn't tell me about the jet. I had to learn about it from Russell Wiggs." He spat out his words, unable to control his anger.

Morgan swallowed hard. Jesse's ego was bruised.

"I-I honestly didn't have time."

"That's a lie, and you know it," he said. "What is the real reason you didn't tell me about flying this morning?"

"I had so much to do to get ready for tonight—"

"For the past three weeks," he cut her off, "I've been getting regular text messages from you every hour of every day. 'Do you prefer white or off-white matte around the photographs?' 'Would you like to create signature packaging to put each photograph into after purchase?' No detail is too small. You leave nothing to chance. Then you're in the flight deck of a jet—and you're too busy to tell me. I'm not buying it, Morgan."

Her stomach dropped. He had a point. "It was a last-minute decision," she stammered in her own defense. "It wasn't a big deal. Until I was up above the clouds that I thought maybe—maybe my life was changing for the better. I took a selfie. I was going to send it to you."

"I thought—" he stopped. "I was wrong."

"Wrong about what?" she asked.

"That you and I had reconnected. But . . ." He rubbed the back of his neck. He wasn't happy with the direction of their conversation. "Right before your parents died on Christmas Eve, you and I sat on this bench and made a commitment. To build a life together. Two days later, you ended it. Without one word." He snapped his fingers.

"I didn't want to drag you into the abyss with me. I'd always fought everyone else's battles. Everyone complimented me on being brave. On being a fighter. But losing my parents . . . it changed everything."

"I would've fought for you. If you'd let me."

"I know you'll never understand the decision I made to

put my family before me. Before us" Her voice was firm and controlled. "I had to do it by myself. I was afraid you'd talk me out of it. I couldn't spend all that money on flight school. I had to make sure Eli and the girls got through college without being saddled with student loan debt."

"Why didn't you ask me for help?"

"It wasn't an option in my mind. I wanted you to go to art school. To follow your dreams wherever they might lead you. Even knowing you'd probably find someone else to share your life."

Jesse was silent, but his body was still tense.

"You won't believe me, but I had every intention of telling you about flying the jet to Chicago. I was hoping you'd be supportive."

"I've spent the last six years of my life trying to figure out a way to move back to Christmas Tree Cove and make a living. I thought maybe you and I had reconnected—" He sighed.

"So, wait. You don't want me to go to the pilot training program? Even though it's my dream." Her determination faltered.

"Of course I want you to be a pilot," he said. He hung his head. "But I don't want you to move away."

"I'm confused, Jesse. Did you think I'd work in your gallery for the rest of my life?"

"No. I—" She was right. He'd been selfish. He'd only considered his own feelings. He didn't have any defense for his actions other than that he'd never been confident in their relationship. She'd never told anyone in her family about her feelings for him. Theirs had always been a secret love.

"I've finally found a way to live in Christmas Tree Cove full time, and you're moving away."

Morgan looked up at him, meeting his gaze. "It's always been my dream, Jesse."

Jesse let go of the breath he'd been holding. "Thank you for telling me the truth. This time."

He shivered. There was a chill in the air, and it had nothing to do with the weather. It was the growing emotional distance between them.

Morgan got to her feet. "I need to get back to the party," she said. "Are you coming?"

"You go ahead. I need a minute," he said.

She started to walk away. Then she turned around. "Merry Christmas, Jesse."

"Merry Christmas, Morgan."

"Maybe we can talk about this again tomorrow," she suggested.

Jesse shook his head. "I'll be in Florida. Skip is flying me to the airport on the three-thirteen."

"Florida?" Morgan was stunned. "You're going to Florida for Christmas?"

Jesse nodded. "You always put your family first." His tone was cold and detached. "Maybe that was a lesson I should've learned from you six years ago."

Her eyes darkened in pain before she turned and walked away without looking back.

Jesse's head dropped into his hands. This was not how he'd expected the gala to end. He was sorry for hurting her. He'd never get over her, but hopefully he could get through this one Christmas without her finding out his heart had shattered into a million pieces again.

Chapter Nineteen

Christmas Eve

THE NEWLY FALLEN snow shimmered like diamonds in the morning sunlight. Morgan was sporting sunglasses, hurrying across the street, toting two coffees in a cardboard carrier and a paper bag of fresh, hot cinnamon buns. She wasn't up for driving all over the county today. She wanted to pull her coverlet over her head and stay in bed, but she'd promised Mrs. Kimura she'd help her deliver terrariums and she didn't want to let her down.

She put up a hand to shield her face from the sun, feeling more sensitive than usual to the bright light, since she'd been awake all night tossing and turning, going back and forth over her argument with Jesse. Her heart shattered over and over like an heirloom-glass Christmas ornament every time she remembered his angry words.

Maybe she should have told Jesse about flying with the jet crew to Chicago when she got the call from Skip, but at the time, she didn't realize one flight would end with her wanting to go into the commercial pilot training program. She hadn't even made a firm decision, although she and her sister had talked about nothing else on the flight back to Traverse City. Dacey had been so supportive and encouraging.

Morgan had so many regrets. She should've texted Jesse the selfie from the cockpit. She should've called him and talked to him before he arrived at the party. Then he'd understand how much it meant to her. But something had stopped her. Was she scared of how he'd react? Or was it because she wasn't sure herself? Moving to Chicago was a huge change. It would completely uproot her life. It made her heart beat double-time. Going to the pilot training program would be the fulfillment of a lifelong dream, but leaving Christmas Tree Cove filled her with dread.

She paused for a moment on the front porch to fix a smile on her face, trying to force her emotions into some kind of order. She needed to appear merry and bright in front of Mrs. Kimura—even though she wasn't feeling anything close to that—before she opened the door.

"Treats for the sweet," Morgan called. She left her wet boots in the tray by the door, then dropped her bag and ditched her hat and coat on the bench in the front hall before carrying the breakfast muffins through to the kitchen.

Mrs. Kimura welcomed her with her usual good humor. "You don't know how much I've been looking forward to this all week."

Morgan's smile was fragile but genuine as she took off her sunglasses and set them on the counter to greet Mrs.

Kimura with a big hug.

"Oh my goodness, Morgan," Mrs. Kimura said. "With your hair down, you could be your mom."

"Really?" she asked. A warm glow flowed through her, knowing Mom would be proud of her for continuing this holiday tradition with their neighbor.

Mrs. Kimura nodded. "Some days the resemblance is more remarkable than others, but today you could be her twin."

"Thank you," Morgan said. "I'll take that as a compliment."

"Your mom was a beautiful woman. Especially this time of year. She practically glowed with Christmas spirit."

Together, they stood at the counter, sipping coffee, nibbling on treats, and sharing bits of gossip they'd overheard at the party. Morgan carefully avoided any Jesse-related topics or mentioning him by name. Which was difficult when the party she'd thrown the night before had been for and about him.

"Was Jesse pleased with everything you did? The gallery looked magnificent."

"Yes. I think so."

I've finally found a way to live in Christmas Tree Cove full time, and you're moving away.

Morgan tried to put Jesse's angry words out of her mind, but every time she blinked, within seconds, he was back. All she could see was Jesse's face. Angry. Annoyed. Hurt. And she didn't know what to do or say to make him believe in her again. To make him stay and listen.

When they finished breakfast, Morgan threw the napkins and paper bag in the trash. "I'll carry the terrariums out to the car," she said. "You can organize them in the order of our delivery stops."

"Good idea," Mrs. Kimura said. "You're so good at organizing. That's why Jesse wanted your help getting his business off the ground."

Morgan pasted a fake smile on her face and nodded. She picked up a cardboard box full of glass jars from the sunroom and carried it through the house and out to the minivan parked in the driveway. Mrs. Kimura trailed along behind, using her key fob to unlock it.

When she was busy, she didn't focus on Jesse, so she kept her hands moving as much as possible. It wasn't long before the little glass terrariums filled every inch of Mrs. Kimura's minivan. Morgan slammed the minivan's hatch shut with one hand, balancing her paper cup of coffee in the other. Walking back to the front of the car, she suddenly remembered a very important part of the holiday. "I've been so busy flying the last few runs of the season and working in the gallery, I haven't had a single moment to shop for Christmas presents."

"It's Christmas Eve. Too late for online shopping," Mrs. Kimura said with a shake of her head. "And shopping in the stores downtown will be crazy this afternoon."

"Yes, but here's the really fun part. Kayla wants a handmade Christmas," Morgan said.

"Handmade?" Mrs. Kimura raised her eyebrows.

"When Eli, Kayla, and Dacey all agreed to honor my request to spend one last Christmas together at Hillcrest House, Kayla piped up and said she wanted it to be a 'handmade Christmas,' with gifts that we all make with our own two hands. I really should make an effort to do what she wants."

"Let's set aside three terrariums," Mrs. Kimura said. Then she picked out three of the glass jars from the back of the car and handed them to Morgan to set aside for safekeeping.

"I did help plant some of the moss and winterberries," Morgan said. "So I won't be lying when Kayla asks if I made them with my own two hands."

Morgan took a lid off one of the glass jars she'd set aside, inhaling the distinctive aroma of moss, winterberries, and pine captured under glass in the terrarium. "Heaven," she said.

How many times had she and her mom discussed how much they loved the distinctive fragrance captured in the Christmas terrariums? Too many to count. Morgan fought back tears. She smiled brightly. "Reminds me of my mom."

"Me too," Mrs. Kimura agreed with a smile. "Shall we listen to some Christmas music? Or is that too over the top?"

"No. It sounds like fun." Morgan laughed.

But the Christmas music that came on when Mrs. Kimura turned on the radio was a sad song about being far from home for the holidays, and Morgan's thoughts drifted back to Jesse.

Why didn't you tell me? You flew a jet this morning.

Mrs. Kimura steered the car over Sugar Hill up the back road to Stony Point, where they dropped off a dozen jars at the assisted-living facility. Turning back to the south, they drove all the way down to Cedar Falls, dropping off terrariums as they went. They chatted comfortably as they drove past orchards and fields near Juniper Point. They turned up driveways that took them all the way back into the woods to sprawling homes and stopped at tiny little houses built right next to the road.

"This is the first year I haven't done these deliveries alone since your mom died," Mrs. Kimura said, as they were pulling away from a farmhouse right out of a classic Christmas movie. "It was my favorite holiday tradition. I miss her so much."

"I miss her too," Morgan agreed. "I miss them. I miss them every day. I've been avoiding so many Christmas traditions since they died. I was afraid I'd constantly be tripping over bad memories if I celebrated without them." She released a deep sigh. "I've been crippled with grief for so long. But the truth is, I have more happy memories of us all together than bad."

"Then we'll have to do this again next year. We could

make it our Christmas tradition," Mrs. Kimura said.

"I don't know if I'll be in Christmas Tree Cove next year," Morgan said with a wistful tone in her voice.

"But you'll come home for Christmas, won't you?" Mrs. Kimura asked.

"I hope so." Morgan wasn't certain where she'd be next year, but she hoped she'd be home for Christmas. She smiled and raised her paper coffee cup in the air. "To new Christmas traditions."

"To new traditions," Mrs. Kimura repeated, holding her fist aloft.

Morgan hummed along to the music, attempting to put Jesse out of her mind, but no matter how hard she tried, all she could see was his face flushed with anger.

You're going to the pilot training. You're moving to Chicago.

"I hope you have a wonderful Christmas this year," Mrs. Kimura said.

She'd been so focused on Jesse, she hadn't been following what Mrs. Kimura was saying.

"We were always a Christmas family," she blurted.

"The lights were always on by five o'clock on Christmas morning." Mrs. Kimura smiled. "Even when you were all grown, you still had your mom and dad up before the sun."

"We had a very full slate of activities." Morgan laughed. "We needed every minute of the twenty-four hours on Christmas Day to get it all in."

"Your mom had four kids, and she always tried to have a special moment with each of you guys during Christmas. Dacey helped her decorate the house. Kayla and Eli helped her in the kitchen. But you were always down on the docks with your dad, so you were harder to reach. The tree on Christmas Tree Cove was her connection to you."

Morgan smiled. "Uncovering the history of the tree on Christmas Tree Cove has been a gift. Knowing the tree was about true love means so much to me."

"I hope by now you've figured out who was putting out the tree when you were a kid."

"It was my dad, wasn't it?"

Mrs. Kimura nodded. "A sign of true love."

"I only wish I knew who put the tree out the night Mom and Dad died. Of all the secrets I uncovered about the tree, it really was the one I was most interested in. Still am."

Mrs. Kimura smiled. "Me too."

Morgan sighed deeply, letting her happy Christmas memories flood her with a warmth that radiated through her body. "Even though I know it will never happen again, the floating tree will always be my favorite holiday tradition in Christmas Tree Cove."

Chapter Twenty

JESSE GOT OUT of bed and stood in the shower without turning on the water, looking out at Christmas Tree Cove through the smallest window in the house as the sun pinked the edge of the sky. He'd been up all night. He hadn't closed his eyes. Not once. He'd tossed and turned for hours, staring at the ceiling, hoping to make some kind of sense out of his fight with Morgan.

He was certain of one thing. It was all his fault. He'd completely messed up.

Finally, he showered and got dressed. Only to discover there wasn't any coffee in the kitchen.

"Dammit!" he slammed his hand on the counter. His anger had very little to do with not having coffee.

He walked down to the docks in Fish Village. He stopped outside the gallery, but he didn't go in. He stared up at the photograph of the tree floating on Christmas Tree Cove Morgan had hung in the storefront window display. He'd taken it right after he and Morgan had made plans to spend the rest of their lives together. The night Morgan's parents had died.

He walked around behind the gallery and sat down on the bench. There were so many ghosts in Fish Village. Generations of fisherman who'd worked before him. Morgan's parents. Charter boat captains. Bush pilots. All of them had probably rested on that bench at some point or another. But alone in Fish Village on Christmas Eve all he could hear was his own angry words echoing in his ears.

He took his time walking home through the downtown shopping district. For the last few days it had been bustling with people but now was still and quiet. Lights had been strung from one side of the street to the other, connecting the two-story brick storefronts on Main Street with festive decorations. Christmas was almost here. Jesse couldn't have cared less.

Pops was making breakfast when he got back to the house.

"There isn't any coffee," Pops said.

"I know."

He sat across the kitchen table while Pops ate. Jesse wasn't hungry, and he wasn't able to pretend he was.

"Does she know you're leaving today?" Pops asked without looking up from his scrambled eggs.

Jesse hesitated. "Yes."

"When is she moving to Chicago?"

"I don't know," he said. "I didn't let her tell me she was considering going to commercial pilot training before I voiced my strong objections."

Pops made a face. "I hope you don't wonder too long why she's angry with you."

Jesse grimaced. "I've said I'm sorry too many times."

Pops swallowed his last bite of eggs. "You gonna let her go? After all this time? You fought for her. You won her back. And now you're gonna let go? Just like that?"

Jesse rubbed a hand across his chin. "It's not 'just like that.' We can't figure it out. We're never in synch. I don't know what else to do. Maybe we're not destined to be together."

"Tell her how you feel."

"She knows."

"You're sure?"

"Yep."

"Maybe you need to say it again."

Jesse patted him on the hand. "Please don't worry too much about it, Pops. I'll be fine. So will she. Eventually."

Morgan needed to go to Chicago. She needed to learn to fly. He'd been encouraging her to make changes in her life. And he needed to go to Florida.

The last thing he wanted was to fly to Florida to spend Christmas on the beach with his parents. When he closed his eyes, he could see the turquoise blue of the water. It was probably somebody's idea of paradise. Not his. Florida was in the opposite direction of where his heart wanted to be. He didn't want to go, but he'd promised his mom. So he packed his bags.

He was an hour early when he arrived in the harbor to check in for the last flight out. Skip greeted him with a curt nod.

"Anybody else flying out this afternoon?" Jesse asked.

"Nope. You're the only fool crazy enough to leave here on Christmas Eve," Skip said. "Maybe, just maybe, you should apologize to her instead."

Jesse was stunned. "Does everyone in Christmas Tree Cove know my business?"

"Only the people who were at the grand opening of the gallery last night," Skip said.

"Everyone was there."

"And that's who knows your business," Skip confirmed.

Jesse pushed his glasses up his nose and sat down on the bench with an air of defeat. "Have you ever spent Christmas anywhere other than Christmas Tree Cove?"

Skip looked unabashed. "I didn't grow up in Christmas Tree Cove."

"You didn't?" Jesse was surprised. Skip was a fixture in the harbor. He'd been flying planes in and out of Christmas Tree Cove since he and Morgan were kids. He was certain Skip's family went back several generations.

"Oh hell no," Skip said. "I was born in Stony Point. Back then the hospital was the building where the VFW Hall is now, so I always like to tell people I was born a veteran."

Jesse laughed. His muscles in his neck and shoulders relaxed a bit. "Stony Point? That's only six miles up the coast."

"Still makes me a non-native, but after all these years I'm happy I call Christmas Tree Cove my home."

Jesse crossed his arms over his chest. "Me too."

"You don't look exactly happy about it." Skip grimaced. "Looks like you're in a tough spot."

"I think we've established I had a rough night."

"I like to talk my troubles over with someone when I'm feeling like that. Someone who'll listen. Someone who ain't judgmental. Someone who'll do almost anything to make sure you're a success. Like organize a grand opening gala and make sure everyone you know shows up to celebrate. You know anyone like that?" Skip's voice was heavy with sarcasm.

"Okay. I get it. You've painted a vivid picture."

"You're born with family. You get to choose your friends. But you have to stick by both—through thick and thin."

"Can we leave now?" Jesse was growing impatient. "If I'm the only passenger."

"When you're wrong, you're wrong. No making it right. It's best to get gone. I'll finish up in the office and then we'll be off."

"Thank you."

Jesse got to his feet and walked off some nervous energy, pacing back and forth on the dock in front of the float plane. A blast of bitterly cold air off the lake left him gasping for air. He closed his eyes. When he opened them, Eli Adair was standing in front of him, holding two paper cups of coffee.

"Hey," Eli said.

"What are you doing here?" Jesse asked. "Please don't tell me you're flying out on the three-thirteen."

"I'm not going anywhere," Eli said. "Here, I brought you a coffee."

"Where did you get this?" Jesse took a sip. "The elixir of the gods."

"If you're nice to the lady who works afternoons in the bookstore, she'll make you a cup of fantastic pour-over coffee."

"Good to know." Jesse filed the information away for a day when he was desperate for caffeine.

"Have you talked to Morgan?" Eli asked, taking a moment to shake fresh snow off his hair and shoulders, most closely resembling a golden retriever after a bath.

"Today?" Jesse shook his head. "No. We don't need to 'talk.' We're fine."

"Right," Eli grinned. "You both looked totally 'fine' last night."

Jesse made a face. "Does everyone in Christmas Tree Cove know we had words?"

Eli nodded. "Pretty much."

Jesse closed his eyes. The truth hurt. "I said something really stupid to her. I don't deny it. But for Morgan to get what she wants, she needs to leave Christmas Tree Cove. To get what I want, I need to come home. Your sister lives in her world. I live in mine. There are no overlapping circles in the Venn diagram that is our lives."

Eli groaned.

"What?" Morgan asked.

"I didn't say anything," Eli protested.

"You made a sound," Jesse said. "It wasn't a nice one."

"Look, it's your business. Although if I might make one tiny observation, you guys are a perfect pair. Morgan needs to learn to fly, and you need to learn to fight."

Jesse guffawed. "I never learned to fight because your sister fought all my battles for me. We spent all our time making up excuses to sneak around together—"

"While the rest of us pretended not to notice." Eli snorted. "You guys were always drawn to each other like magnets. You're perfect for each other."

"I used to think so." Jesse crossed his arms over his chest. "Skip? Are we leaving soon?"

Skip stuck his head out of the office. "I'll be right along. I need to check the weather again. Looks like it's snowing pretty good in Traverse City."

"Keep me posted." Jesse was impatient and irritable, wishing Eli would leave him alone. Instead Morgan's brother sat down next to him on the bench.

"Can I run something by you?" Eli asked. "About Hillcrest House."

"You want to run something by me? Seriously? I'm Jesse Taylor, remember?"

"Yeah. You're a pretty questionable risk as a potential

mate for my sister, but there's no denying you've turned your dream of being a freelance photographer into a very successful business."

"Thanks," Jesse said. "I think."

Eli took a sip of coffee. "Six years ago, when our parents died Morgan didn't hesitate before she sacrificed everything she loved for me, Kayla, and Dacey. She gave up the flight training program and stayed here. She was our rock. And when we started to move on, you can imagine our surprise when we discovered that our rock was stuck—unable to move or go anywhere. It was heartbreaking. Her pain was so palpable. I started to avoid coming home. Dacey did too. But Morgan put her foot down and insisted. I almost said no, selfish bastard that I am. That's part of the reason why I pushed so hard to put the house on the market. We had to do something—anything—to shake things up in her world. To get Morgan unstuck."

Jesse shook his head. "But I should've—"

"I'm going to buy Hillcrest House," Eli cut him off. "I'm going to buy my sisters out. Dacey and Kayla both need the money. And Morgan will need it too. Pilot training is expensive. So is living in Chicago."

"You're going to move back to Christmas Tree Cove and live in that big old house all by yourself?" Jesse shook his head. "You're crazy."

"I need a change. The timing is right. Wren Williams is selling some of her family's property up on Sugar Hill. I found a spot with a view of the harbor. I want to open up a seasonal beer garden."

"A beer garden?" Jesse asked. "It's a great idea. But I don't understand. Why are you telling me this? Where do I fit in?"

"When I said Morgan sacrificed everything she loved to make sure my sisters and I would get through school and have what we needed to launch ourselves into a happy life, I was talking about *you*," Eli said. "She sacrificed you. She loved you. You were the center of her world, and she cut you completely out of her life to help us. Must've really hurt."

Jesse closed his eyes. It wasn't what he'd expected to hear Eli say. Not by a long shot, but he was right.

"Morgan loved you. She was all in. Still does, from what I can tell. And I'm assuming you have feelings too."

Jesse nodded. "I love her. I've always loved her. But I can't seem to get out of my own way long enough to prove it to her."

Eli rubbed his hand through his hair. "When you asked her to set up a gallery in Fish Village, I figured we were on the same page. She needed to chase a few ghosts away down there. But I can only speculate as to what might've happened at the party last night."

"I was an ass," Jesse said. "And forgot to say, 'I'm sorry.'"

"Love is complicated," Eli said. "Which is why I don't play that game. You're a braver man than I am. But honestly, Morgan organized the business you said you wanted and threw you a grand opening gala. If that isn't an act of true love and devotion, what is it?"

Jesse swallowed hard. "Then she announced she was moving away from Christmas Tree Cove at the party."

"There was no announcement. You overheard a rumor and made some not so good assumptions," Eli smacked him down.

"Gah." Jesse made a sound as if he'd been punched in the gut.

"You went away to art school. And you've done everything you can to work your way back here," Eli said. "Where she's been waiting. Like a rock. Now she needs you to be her rock."

"Her rock," Jesse repeated Eli's words. Why had it taken him so long to get a clear picture of his own situation?

"If you think it's possible you could play that role for her in the immediate future," Eli said, pulling a package out of the kangaroo pocket on his sweatshirt and shoving it across the bench, "then this will help you when you take the next step."

Jesse recognized the well-worn, dark-velvet ring box. He'd given it back to Eli six years ago for safekeeping. "What's my next step?"

Eli shrugged. "That's not my purview. I'm guessing you'll need to grovel big-time. Get it all out in the open. Tell the world, 'I love this woman. This one right here. Always and forever.' But if you stepped in it last night as badly as you say you did, you'll need more than an antique engagement ring to convince her you're for real."

"You're right. Got any ideas?"

"We're talking about a massive grand gesture. Your feelings on display with no ambiguity. Or else your heart will be irreversibly broken."

"Massive?" Jesse asked.

Eli cocked his head. "Morgan would probably settle for the ring," he said. "But since she's my sister, I want to see you fight for her like she always did for you."

Just then, Skip reappeared on the dock. "You talk him out of going to Florida yet?"

"I made my case," Eli said.

"I hope so. I never fueled the plane."

"Is that why you tried to convince me to stay here for Christmas?" Jesse asked.

"It's snowing pretty hard downstate. I figured you'd come to your senses eventually," Skip said. "I'll drive you to the airport myself if you still want to go. But I'll tell you that you're crazy every chance I get."

"I've got a better idea," Jesse said with a wicked smile. He radiated a sense of calm and self-confidence. He was absolutely certain of what he needed to do.

"You're gonna talk to Morgan." Skip's happy-go-lucky optimism had returned.

"Well. Yeah, but no," Jesse said. "I've bungled this very badly. I'm gonna need some help." He crossed his arms over his chest and fixed them both with a pointed look. "We're going to need a boat."

Eli high-fived Skip while Jesse got to his feet.

"You're in luck." Eli grinned. "I've got a hookup with a deputy sheriff."

Chapter Twenty-One

MORGAN NAVIGATED THE snowdrifts in the driveway and entered Hillcrest House through the kitchen door. No one was more surprised than she was to find Kayla and Dacey in mid-conversation at the table with a bottle of red wine and two half-full balloon wineglasses. Crackers, cheese, olives, and mixed nuts were scattered over a wooden serving plank, but the conversation came to a complete halt the moment Morgan appeared.

"Are you okay?" Kayla asked. She was dressed for church in a soft cardigan and plaid skirt. Her hair fell in soft layers around her face. It was an entirely different style from her usual I'm-a-super-busy-art-teacher uniform: jeans, T-shirt, her sun-streaked hair barely contained in a scrunchie.

Morgan looked away. Kayla's gaze searched her face for signs of distress.

Morgan had taken a walk around the block on her way home from the Kimuras'. She didn't want her siblings to know her heart was broken. Without a mirror, she had no idea if her face was streaked with telltale mascara.

"Is something wrong?" Dacey prompted. She, too, had

taken the time to put on makeup and brush her hair until it was shiny. In a smart-looking, blush wool sweater and matching pants, she looked like a chic and stylish urbanite who'd stepped out of *Elle* magazine.

"I'm fine." Keeping her face hidden, Morgan half-turned to her sisters, unable to make eye contact. "Where's Eli?"

Dacey shrugged. "He went out this afternoon. He's not answering texts."

"No doubt he's trying to avoid going to Christmas Eve service." Kayla laughed.

"I'm going to change. I'll be right back." Without another word, Morgan sprinted toward the stairs.

In her tower room, she pulled on her new gray wool pants and matching cardigan. She added a pop of color with the jade necklace her dad had brought her from a fancy department store in San Francisco. He'd said it matched her eyes. Then she finished with her high-heeled boots.

She did her best artwork to cover the dark circles under her eyes and added some red lipstick as a decoy. Then she jogged back down the stairs.

Hillcrest House was glowing with Christmas cheer. Eli put up a tree in the living room that was tall enough to scrape the ceiling. Dacey had put together the Olde English Christmas village Mom had collected since they were little on the fireplace mantel. Rushing through the dining room to rejoin her sisters in the kitchen, Morgan stopped to admire Kayla's handmade balsam-and-winterberry centerpiece.

"Still no word from Eli?" Morgan asked. "I'll text him. He can't ignore all of us."

"Yes, he can," Dacey said. "He's really good at ignoring stuff he doesn't want to do."

"Jeff isn't responding to texts either," Kayla said, crossing her arms over her chest.

"This is all a ploy to get out of going to church."

"Whatever it is, they better have a really good story."

Morgan grabbed a glass from the cabinet and filled it with wine, then pulled up a chair in front of the charcuterie platter. "Maybe we should let them have the night off. It's Christmas Eve, after all."

Her sisters shared a look. "What's up with you?" Kayla asked.

Dacey scrutinized Morgan's face. "What happened?"

"I'm fine. I'll be fine." Morgan took a sip of wine. Then she paused and took a deep breath. "You know how every year on Christmas Eve a floating Christmas tree always appeared in the harbor?

Kayla nodded. "You and Mom used to stay up all night watching until the lights went out."

"Did you ever notice Dad never went to church on Christmas Eve?" Morgan asked.

Dacey grinned. "He always said he had to stay home and wrap his Christmas gifts."

"Right. Did you ever see the presents he wrapped?" Kayla insisted. "How long did that actually take?"

"Fifteen minutes. Dad was crap at wrapping," Dacey confirmed.

"He wasn't wrapping presents," Kayla agreed. "He was getting out of going to church."

"Not exactly," Morgan said. "I've been doing a bit of 'Nancy Drew' sleuthing about the history of the Christmas Eve tree. Mom probably did, too, when she first got married and moved here. She wouldn't have to go too far to discover her neighbor was putting out the tree to honor his wife."

"Mr. Kimura?"

Morgan nodded. "When they first moved here from San Francisco, Mrs. Kimura was homesick. By the time we were born, Mr. Kimura was getting older. He must've asked Dad for help at some point."

"What are you saying?" Kayla asked.

Morgan grinned. "I don't exactly know when, but at some point, Dad took over and started putting the tree out in the harbor ever year on Christmas Eve. For Mom."

"It was Dad? All those years? Are you sure?"

Morgan nodded. "It's nice to know, isn't it? The tree was a physical representation of their love for all to see."

"I wish we'd known sooner," Kayla said.

"Me too," Morgan said.

"For me, the floating tree was always a celebration of being home for the holidays," Dacey said. "Knowing Mom and Dad were involved makes me believe—"

"In true love," Kayla finished her sentence.

"And hope," Morgan said.

Dacey shook her head. "I can't imagine being that head over heels for someone."

"I can." Morgan's voice was as soft as a whisper.

"You?" Dacey asked.

Kayla smiled. "We're talking about Jesse Taylor, am I right?"

Morgan nodded. "He was my best friend in high school. We didn't hang out, but he was the one person I told all my secrets to. We actually dated in college. And we were going to move to Chicago together, but then . . . the accident."

"Wait. You were moving to Chicago together?"

Morgan nodded. "I tried to forget him. I told myself that he'd moved on, that no matter what happened, I'd be all right without him. But then we kissed, and everything changed."

"Wait. Have you kissed Jesse recently?"

Morgan's face flamed with heat. "I . . . we . . . maybe."

"Why am I always the last to know everything?" Dacey asked. "Tell us what it's like to kiss Jesse Taylor? Spare no detail."

"It's like . . ." Morgan stopped. Words were inadequate to describe her feelings about him. Kissing Jesse was better than magic.

"It's like standing on the end of the dock in the harbor after it rains. The air holds the scent of wood smoke and fresh fish. A chill wind is blowing the spicy scent of evergreens down from Sugar Hill. And someone on a nearby boat is making a fresh cup of pour-over coffee, and you take a bite out of a gooey, fresh-from-the-oven cinnamon roll the size of your head." Morgan stopped to consider for a moment. "That's it. That's what it's like to kiss Jesse Taylor."

Silence.

Morgan looked across the table at her sisters. She was pretty sure one or both of them had stopped breathing. Or had been rendered mute.

"Hello," Morgan prompted, waving her hands in front of their faces. "Are you guys still alive?"

Kayla and Dacey exchanged a glance while Dacey struggled to find the right words. "Kissing Jesse sounds—"

"Very adequate, wouldn't you say, Dacey?" Kayla supplied.

Dacey grinned. "Very adequate. Yes. That's it."

Morgan burst out laughing. "I might've oversold it a little. But it's pretty fantastic."

"No, no." Dacey held up her hands in protest. "You didn't. I'm sure. Jesse is hot."

"So we're talking about like the Best Kiss Ever then?" Kayla asked. "Is that what I'm hearing you say?"

Morgan nodded. "Pretty much."

Kayla fanned herself. "I'm feeling that."

"And after kissing you like that, he walked away?"

Morgan nodded. "His family is in Florida for Christmas."

"Huh. Not what I expected from him. A kiss like that, he should really be your ride or die. Especially after everything you guys have been through."

Morgan smiled, but she was still feeling a bit teary. "I always believed if people reconnect like we did, then their story is destined to have a happily ever after ending, but I was wrong."

"It's true. Odds are against it," Dacey agreed.

"The professor has spoken," Kayla teased. "Anyway—the whole thing with Jesse doesn't matter anymore. He made his choice and you're moving on."

Morgan nodded. "I'm trying not to . . . well, it's Christmas Eve. Mom always said I should be counting my blessings. And right off the top of my head, I can think of two." She pointed to her sisters and smiled.

Kayla checked her watch. "I'm getting worried about Eli and Jeff. Why aren't they texting any of us back?"

"If we don't leave now, we're going to end up in the balcony by the choir loft."

"Those are the most uncomfortable pews in the church."

"I'm going to text Jeff and tell him to meet us there," Kayla said.

THE LITTLE CHURCH they'd attended since they were children was filled with candles, covering every flat surface in the main sanctuary. The candlelit room was filled to capacity by the time they arrived, so an usher directed them to the balcony. On their way up the stairs, Dacey snagged a couple of cookies off the table set up for after the service. Morgan burst into giggles. Her sister was incorrigible.

They slid into the pew just as the organist was hitting the opening notes of "Silent Night."

The three sisters didn't need a hymnal to follow the lyrics. Rising to their feet with the rest of the congregation, Morgan, Dacey, and Kayla sang as if they were filled with the spirit of Christmas.

"Why am I always in the middle?" Dacey complained.

"We're seated by birth order," Kayla said.

"Could you guys please be quiet?" Morgan begged. "We're in church."

When they were little, Mom never let them sit next to each other in church. She physically separated each of her daughters with the other people in the family. Mom took Morgan. Dad had Kayla, while Dacey and Eli were allowed to sit nearby and read books. In high school, Morgan and Kayla gave each other the giggles until they were gasping for air but helpless to stop.

Tonight was different. On this, the most holy of nights, Morgan said a prayer for her parents. She thanked God for her siblings and friends. And last, but not least, she asked for a blessing for Jesse.

I love Jesse with all my heart. If only he believed in me the way I believe in him.

Chapter Twenty-Two

CHRISTMAS TREE COVE was living up to its name. With big fluffy snowflakes falling from the sky, it was like a winter fairyland. Jeff and Eli stood on the dock next to the sheriff's patrol boat, waiting like soldiers for their instructions from Jesse.

"Okay. This less-than-perfect part of the plan has two stages. First, we need to procure the tree and the decorations," he said.

"We need a Christmas tree. It's important. Why didn't I think of it sooner?" Eli asked.

"Where are we going to get one on Christmas Eve?" Skip interrupted. "All the stores are closed."

"I think all the materials we need are hidden," Jesse assured them with confidence. "Inside the old Adair family boathouse."

"You're probably right," Eli said. "Let's go."

"Wait. One thing before we go. Even if we do manage to pull this off, you guys can never tell anyone about it. Ever," Jesse issued the direst of warnings again. "It will have to be our little secret forever."

"Oh, I don't like the sound of this," Skip said. "I don't like it at all."

"Me neither," Eli said. "And I'm so all in."

"Me too."

Jeff shot Eli a dirty look. "You promised me it wouldn't be illegal."

"I promised we wouldn't break the law tonight," Eli said. "And so far, so good."

The small group scrambled into the sheriff's patrol boat. Jeff positioned himself behind the wheel. Jesse wished Morgan were here. She was always the one chosen to drive the boat when they went water skiing. Her confidence and her steady hand at the wheel meant she was able to steer a boat even when variables like wind and waves threw everything out of balance.

"I keep getting text messages from Kayla," Jeff said.

"Me too," Eli said. "I'm getting texts from all three of my sisters. Maybe it's time to turn off our phones." The others nodded in agreement.

Jeff piloted the sheriff's boat with skill, which was especially difficult at night. Within fifteen minutes he had navigated the narrow channel of Fish Village and pulled alongside the Adairs' old boathouse.

"The boathouse should be empty," Jesse said.

Eli nodded. "No one in our family has used it in years." He hopped out to pull lines and tie up the boat securely to the pilings at the fore and aft. Jeff cut the engine and joined

Jesse on the dock.

"It's padlocked," Skip said, shining a flashlight over the metal brackets holding the doors closed.

"That's unexpected," Jesse said.

"We're not going to have to break in, are we?" Jeff asked. He sounded worried.

Eli shook his head. "The lock on the boathouse is for display purposes only. It's been broken for years."

Eli lifted the padlock off the metal hasp holding the doors closed, and the wide wooden doors swung open. He and Jesse searched the walls for the light switch while Skip helped Jeff expertly back up the boat into the bay.

"Jesse, give me a leg up. I'll get the tree and the stand from the rafters. I'm sure that's where Dad kept it," Eli said. "Skip, grab the timer and the lights from the workbench. If we work fast, we can have the tree decorated and ready to tow out on the dive raft into the harbor in a half hour."

"It's freezing out here," Skip added. "And it's not going to be any warmer out on the cove."

"Let's get a move on," Jesse said. He and Skip scrambled to attach the dive raft to the boat, but the dive raft was listing at a thirty-degree angle in the water and the wooden decking underneath had sunk beneath the water.

"This raft has seen better days," Jesse said.

He took a tentative step onto the dive raft and fell through the rotted wood into water up to his knees. Fast-thinking Skip and Eli quickly came to his rescue, but the raft was irreversibly damaged.

"The drums have separated from the rotten wooden slats," Jesse confirmed with a flashlight.

"We had many summers of fun jumping off that raft, but it's not seaworthy," Eli said.

"That throws a wrench into an already very-badly-thought-out plan," Jesse said.

"What are we going to do now?" Jeff asked.

"You guys are overlooking the obvious. It's right there in Fish Village. *Hope*. She's been tied up on the docks behind the *Dorthea Lou* to create a photo op for tourists for years."

"The little red dinghy? It's perfect. It's almost identical to the one used for the original floating tree," Eli said.

"I can't believe she still floats."

"That solves one of our problems. We still have one major hurdle to face," Jesse said. He gestured in the direction of the fake Christmas tree. "That is not going to fit in the *Hope*."

"Good point," Eli said.

"Where are we going to get a tree on Christmas Eve?" Skip asked. "The Christmas tree market is closed."

"We could steal one from someone's front porch," Eli said with a grin.

"I didn't hear that," Jeff said.

"Wait. I've got an idea. Eli, come with me. Skip, you stay with Jeff in the boat. We'll be right back," Jesse said.

When they returned to Fish Village a half hour later,

there was a fully decorated, tiny Christmas tree in his truck bed. He and Eli carried it between them down to the dock.

"It's the perfect size for the *Hope*. Where'd you get that?" Skip asked.

"My mother's living room. I was supposed to water it, but I forgot."

Skip covered his laugh with his hand. "If this doesn't work, you're going to be in big trouble."

"Either way, I'm going to be in trouble," Jesse said.

Jeff checked his iPhone. "We are too. We are not going to make any of the church service."

"I'm totally fine with that," Eli said.

"Me too." Jeff grinned.

"Someone is going to have to hold on to the painter of the dinghy while we pull her along behind us," Eli noted. "Jesse? Are you okay with that?"

"Maybe now would be a good time to mention I am not a strong swimmer."

"Seriously, you grew up on Lake Michigan. On a fishing tug. Why didn't you learn to swim?" Skip asked.

Jesse shrugged and stepped into the dinghy with the tree. "Be gentle and take it slow," he said.

With Jeff at the helm, they towed the dinghy with the tree and Jesse out of Fish Village and into the main harbor. When they got closer to the break wall, Jeff slowed the boat while Skip climbed into the front of the patrol boat and used a flashlight to search the dark water.

"What are you looking for?" Eli asked.

"The buoy. It's out here somewhere. I'm not sure of the exact spot." It was like looking for a small tropical island in the middle of the Pacific. In the dark. With a cold wind blowing snow out of the west and whipping up waves on the normally calm surface of the harbor.

"This would be so much easier if Morgan was here." Skip crossed his arms over his chest. "She knows every inch of Christmas Tree Cove."

"She can navigate this harbor blindfolded." Eli was leaning over the side, also trying to locate the orange buoy. "I'm an amateur—wait, there it is."

"I see it," Jeff shouted, waving from behind the helm.

"All we have to do is attach the dinghy. And we're done."

It wasn't as easy as it looked. In the end, Jesse had to crawl over the Christmas tree to tie off the painter to the anchor's buoy, but the third time was the charm. Jesse was huddled in the bottom of the dingy for an eternity, fiddling with the timer and the lights. By the time he was ready to get back in the sheriff's boat, his teeth were chattering.

Taking a wide step to get back onboard the patrol boat, he slipped and dragged his one dry foot through the water. Eli and Skip quickly pulled him up onto the deck. Even so, the frigid water of Lake Michigan left Jesse gasping for breath.

"Gotta tell you," Eli said with a shiver as a brisk breeze blew in from the west, causing a little ripple in the waves, "when I signed up for this gig, I had no idea it would be so cold."

"And wet," Jesse agreed.

"Ok. Everybody safely back on board?" Jeff asked.

"All hands present and accounted for. Let's go," Jesse said. Jeff hit the engine and they sped back to the harbor. Within a few minutes, the sheriff's boat was in the slip where they'd found it. Jeff tucked the boat key back into its hiding place on a nail under the dock.

They hurried toward the harbor parking lot, looking vaguely suspicious. It wasn't until they were safely gathered around their trucks that the men shared high fives all around.

"That was the most fun I've ever had on Christmas Eve," Jeff said with uncharacteristic good humor.

"We should do this every year," Skip agreed.

Jesse grinned. "This may be the revival of a great holiday tradition in Christmas Tree Cove."

He waved goodbye to Skip and then got in his truck. As Eli and Jeff were pulling out of the parking lot, Eli rolled down the window. "What time did you set on the timer?" he asked.

"Ten o'clock. That's when the evening church services are scheduled to end," Jesse said. "I'm going to go home and change, then come back to the harbor. I've set the trap. Now all I have to do is wait."

"Good luck," Eli said.

"Thanks for everything. I mean it," Jesse said. A strange kind of numb comfort radiated through his body. It had nothing to do with the fact that he was wet from the knees down and his toes were in the early stages of frostbite.

TWO HOURS LATER, Jesse prowled the docks in Fish Village. The quiet assurance he'd been feeling earlier had disappeared as a wave of apprehension gnawed away at his confidence. Jesse checked his iPhone. It was two minutes past the hour. The lights on the tree should've come on by now.

This was crazy.

He should've apologized in person. What if Morgan didn't see the tree? What if she didn't go to church?

And what if the lights on the tree never turned on? All of their efforts would be for nothing. He peered out over the water, searching the darkness for the tree lights.

His anxiety was beginning to amp up to a new level when he suddenly heard the sound of Christmas carols. Floating on the cold night air, the music sounded as if it was coming from the town square. No one had mentioned anything about carols on Christmas Eve. Didn't that usually happen earlier in the season? He looked over his shoulder at the lights near the center of town.

Then he turned back to the harbor.

His breath caught in his throat.

Just like magic, it had appeared. The little tree in the dinghy covered in brightly lit Christmas lights was floating in the harbor. The scrawny pine tree that had looked so pathetic in his mother's living room looked almost regal in the tiny dinghy.

He exhaled a deep sigh, smiling broadly at the tree. He was now a part of a long-standing tradition of true love and devotion. He only had one question on his mind. Had everyone who'd ever floated a tree in Christmas Tree Cove been so fidgety with excitement and anticipation while waiting for their efforts to be acknowledged by their true love?

As was his habit, Jesse snapped off some pictures. His mood was suddenly buoyant. The stars were shining in the night sky, and the Christmas lights were reflecting on the water.

All he could do now was wait. His fate totally depended on *Hope*.

Chapter Twenty-Three

WHEN THE CHOIR finished singing the last hymn, the pastor stood in front of the congregation for a final announcement.

"We are gathered here tonight to celebrate Christmas. I'm always glad to see so many familiar faces in the church. For many of you, going to church on the night before Christmas is a tradition."

He paused to smile at one of the children in the front row, but his attention was drawn to the balcony where Eli and Jeff were now arriving fifteen minutes before the end of the service. As soon as they sat down they endured dirty looks from all three of the Adair sisters.

"Could my husband be more suspicious?" Kayla responded.

Morgan covered her giggle with her hand as the pastor continued to address the congregation. "I've talked to a lot of people who've expressed how sad it is that the tradition of the floating Christmas Eve tree is now a part of our history. In many ways, the tree was the essence of this community," he said. "And so tonight, I want to start a new tradition in

Christmas Tree Cove."

"Our children's choir is going to lead us out of the church. We're going to walk up the block to the town square where we will meet up with the congregations of several other churches who have all coordinated their services to end at the same time. And together the community of Christmas Tree Cove will come together to sing 'Joy to the World.'"

Tucking her hand into Kayla's elbow, Morgan wrapped her other arm around Dacey's shoulders as they left the church. The night sky above was clear and filled with twinkling stars. Paper bag luminaries had been lit along the sidewalks to guide the congregants from the churches to the town square. People spoke in hushed tones, pointing at the sparkling lights and decorations on the stores along Main Street.

The three sisters waved at people they'd known all their lives, bidding "Merry Christmas" to the others they hadn't seen before tonight. Everyone they met was filled with the spirit of the season.

"What a beautiful night." Kayla sighed. "Now that the snowstorm has passed, there isn't a cloud in the sky."

"I am always amazed at how many stars I can see when I'm in Christmas Tree Cove," Dacey agreed. "In the city, I can't find more than two stars that make up the Big Dipper."

Morgan smiled. "Maybe you guys need to come back to Christmas Tree Cove more often. The sky is as big and beautiful in the summer too. And there are just as many stars."

"You may be right." Dacey giggled.

"I'm glad you insisted we get together in the house again," Kayla added. "Even though it's moments like this when I miss Mom and Dad the most."

Morgan hugged her sister tighter.

"Mom would've loved this. Gathering to sing in the town square," Kayla said.

"Dad would be grumbling about too much peopling, while waving and shouting 'Merry Christmas' to everyone in sight," Morgan said, making her sisters laugh.

Arriving at the town square, the Adair family and the other members of their church merged with several other local congregations. Morgan studied the faces in the crowd, hoping to find Jesse. For six years, she'd searched every crowded location in order to avoid him. Now all she wanted was to see him again. She wanted to apologize. She wanted to start over.

Count your blessings.

Morgan took a deep breath. She needed to enjoy this Christmas Eve with her brother and sisters. A night like this may never happen again.

Jesse.

If only she'd had a chance to tell him about flying. If only the news hadn't been sprung on him by someone else as soon as he walked in the door. Maybe he would've listened to her instead of being angry. If only . . .

Stop. That's magical thinking. It won't change anything.

Jesse had made his choice. He'd gone to Florida to be with his family for Christmas. And her brother and sisters had all come home to have Christmas at Hillcrest House. If ever there was a time to count her blessings, it was this Christmas Eve.

She pulled Dacey closer. Kayla looped her arm through hers. Standing arm in arm with her sisters, Morgan's heart was filled to overflowing with love. She grinned at Eli, who was distracted by something in the harbor. But that was Eli. He was always distracted. It was part of his charm.

She said a silent prayer of gratitude that all her siblings were in Christmas Tree Cove on this night. Then one of the choir directors stepped up into the gazebo. "Please join your friends and neighbors in singing 'Joy to the World.'"

The crowd was boisterous and enthusiastic, so loud Morgan was certain they'd woken up all of Wisconsin and Canada with their off-key warbling. In the middle of the second chorus, one of the kids goofing around near Eli shouted, "Look! On Christmas Tree Cove!"

He pointed to the water.

As the singing slowly came to a stop, a hush swept over the crowd. Morgan turned and looked over her shoulder. Her breath caught in her throat.

A lighted Christmas tree was floating in the harbor in the antique dinghy called *Hope*. Shining like a beacon of holiday cheer, the lights from the little tree reached up into the sky as if to touch the North Star that guided the magi to adore the newborn Jesus the Christ on the night he was born.

"Oh, look," Dacey said, turning back to sneak a peek over her shoulder. "Mom's tree is back."

"It's beautiful," Kayla said.

"It's magical," Morgan said, wrapping her sisters in a group hug.

"I wonder if Jeff and Eli had anything to do with it?" Kayla asked.

"I wonder," Morgan said. Then she untangled herself. "I've got to go."

"Where are you going?" Dacey asked.

She pressed a finger to her lips. "It's a secret."

Her sisters nodded waved goodbye. Morgan walked with purposeful long strides along Main Street. She broke into a run in the deserted harbor parking lot, hurrying until she reached the end of the docks. Morgan tucked the ends of her scarf into her coat and wrapped the knitted fabric across her face. The night air was exceptionally chilly and brisk. The toes of her boots hung a few inches over the last of the wooden slats.

The water was calm and crystal clear. The mirrored surface reflected the lights on the tree throughout the harbor. The sky above was a painting of black velvet, lit by a universe of stars, but Morgan's entire focus was on the tree floating in the tiny dinghy. A scrawny tree that had probably never gotten enough sunlight to grow tall and straight was covered in bright-colored lights. A proud symbol of the holidays. And the love of a good man.

For Morgan, the mystery of why there was a floating Christmas tree in the harbor had been solved. It was a sign of enduring love, and it was there for her.

Her heart was overflowing with joy. When Hillcrest House was sold and a new family was living in the house on the cliff, the tree floating in the harbor on Christmas Eve would forever be her connection to her mom.

Wrapping her arms around her torso in an effort to calm herself, Morgan took a deep breath and spoke her truth out loud.

"Mama." Morgan's voice little more than a hoarse whisper. "It doesn't seem like a real Christmas. Not without you. Not without Dad. But we're here. All four of us. I don't know what the future holds. I don't know when we'll spend Christmas together again, but you'd be proud of us. We've stayed together as a family. We miss you. And Dad. So much."

Morgan stopped and took another deep breath.

"Six years ago, I would've started this conversation by asking, 'Why you? Why both of you? Why did you have to die?' It took me three years to stop thinking about you constantly. I've been going through the motions of life, but not really living. Your love is unchanged in my heart, but I can't keep my life unchanged. I've tried, but everything is different now that you're gone.

"I wish I'd solved the mystery of the floating tree long ago. I wished I'd known its secrets while you were still alive. It took me all this time to figure it out, but I am glad to finally know.

"The thing is . . ." She choked and had to take a moment before she could continue. "Since you blessed me with life, I want to honor the love you shared. More than anything else, it's a life I want. With someone who loves me. In the same way you unconditionally loved each other."

Morgan hesitated. "I love Jesse Taylor. Very much. And he loves me. I know this because I've tested his love. Too many times to count. My love for him is unconditional. Constant. Never-ending."

Suddenly her voice was drowned out by another chorus of "Joy to the World." The joyful sound of Christmas carols drifting across the water—there was no better soundtrack for her at this moment.

"Merry Christmas. It won't be the same without you, but at least when the floating tree appears here on Christmas Tree Cove every year, I'll always know you're close by."

Morgan turned around and took the path to Fish Village from the harbor, smiling at each familiar plank as she stepped on them on her way. Halfway up the dock, standing in front of the sign over the door of the art gallery, she could see someone in the shadows.

Impossibly tall. Lanky. Slightly awkward. The kind of guy who'd get picked last for dodgeball and always had a camera on a leather strap around his neck.

Jesse would never be the kind of man to follow anyone else's lead. He did things his own unique way. And so did she. She waved. Jesse waved back.

He would always wait for her. Even when she was lost, it was Jesse who found a way to light up the night to help her out of the darkness. Picking up her steps, she ran toward him, blissfully happy and fully alive for the first time in so very long.

Morgan couldn't see his face in the darkness, but she was certain he was smiling. She smiled knowing he was moving toward her with a slow gait, like someone used to moving at his own pace. He wouldn't be hurried. Wouldn't be scolded. His loose-limbed walk was easy and confident.

In the darkness, she heard the click of a camera, and she hurried toward the sound. She didn't want to waste one more minute of her life without him.

Chapter Twenty-Four

J ESSE CLICKED THE shutter on his camera. To his surprise the star on top of the Christmas tree in the harbor magically lit up with a golden glow, sending radiant light out into the night. The light reflected off the water in the harbor, filling the frame in his camera with brightly colored Christmas lights.

"Wow," Jesse muttered.

It was so dark in the harbor he had the lens set on the lowest aperture to allow as much light as possible to enter the camera. Maybe something had gone wrong. He didn't have time to check the images he'd captured. Morgan was closing the distance between them, and all he wanted in the world was to gather her in her arms and hold on to her.

Morgan stopped inches away from him in front of the Bait & Tackle Co.

"You okay?" she smiled up at him. "You look like you've seen a ghost."

Jesse nodded. "Not a ghost. More like some kind of Christmas miracle."

Morgan crossed her arms over her chest. "What are you

doing here? Why aren't you on the beach in Miami?"

He took a step closer to her. "It's a funny story. I was in the harbor, dreading, as always, getting on a plane, when someone a lot smarter than me pointed out that I was making a huge mistake." He bent close enough for his lips to brush her ear. "I'm so sorry."

She looked into his eyes. "It's not your fault. I should've told you first about my plan, or at least given you a moment to catch your breath before the bomb was dropped."

"No. It's my—"

"Stop." She pressed her hand to the center of his chest. "We're both here now. For the first time in forever, we're together. And it's Christmas Eve. There aren't any obstacles in our path. Let's count our blessings."

He pulled her in for a hug, holding her close to his chest. "I have at least one blessing. You. You have always been my best friend. I've never deserved you."

She smiled. "You're mine. Thank you for waiting for me. For being here. Even if you had some doubts. But what are you doing out here on the docks? It's really cold."

"I'm having a picnic."

He gestured to a wicker picnic basket on the front of the *Faith*. He'd spread out a plaid blanket and had scattered piles of quilts on the foredeck of the tug.

"What's on the menu?" she asked.

"I made popcorn. With butter. And I've got homemade hot cocoa in a thermos."

"Marshmallows?" she asked.

Jesse's heart plunged to his toes. "No one told me about the marshmallows."

Morgan laughed. "I'm kidding about the marshmallows. You planned the menu so perfectly, I wanted to see what you'd say."

He glowered at her, which only made her laugh harder. "Stop messing with me. You're breaking my heart." Her giggles were infectious. "Do you want to join me?" He gestured to the boat.

"Yes." She nodded. He reached for her, pulling her up and over the gap between the dock and the deck of the boat. She took each step in stride.

"Welcome aboard," he said. Jesse didn't protest when she wrapped her arms around his torso. He held her in his arms, pressing a gentle kiss into her hair. He was immediately aware of her delicious scent. She smelled of wildflowers and peppermint, even in the middle of winter.

Jesse guided her to the front of the tug with an arm around her shoulders. Morgan relaxed against his soft flannel shirt, and he let go of a deep sigh.

"I've got some blankets and quilts if you're cold. Wait 'til you see the view of the tree from the forward hold."

She grinned. "This is fun."

They settled together on the deck. He wrapped a blanket around her shoulders and poured hot chocolate into paper cups, then handed one off to her. "Are you warm enough?"

he asked.

She nodded. "I am perfectly perfect."

"Were you surprised when you saw the tree? Or did your brother tell you?"

"Eli?" She scrunched up her nose. "No. Although now that you mention it, I should've been suspicious when he and Jeff showed up late to Christmas Eve service with their pants wet up to their knees."

Jesse laughed and nodded.

"Do you think my mom knew it was my dad putting the tree in the harbor for her every year on Christmas Eve?"

"I'm sure she did," he said. "It was an open secret in Fish Village."

"Huh. Why did she keep it a secret from me?" Morgan said.

"For the same reason we keep the truth about Santa a secret from kids." He flashed a grin. "So that the magic of Christmas lives on in our hearts for as long as possible."

She smiled. "You're probably right."

A cold breeze tickled his cheek. Her nose was as bright red as a cherry. He wrapped her up in another quilt and held her tighter. "Do you want to go inside the gallery to warm up?"

"No." Her mood was as bright as her eyes. "I'm not leaving until the lights go out."

Jesse needed to tell her more about what happened on Christmas Eve six years ago, but he was still gathering his thoughts. He moved so he could see the glow from the lights on the tree reflected in her eyes. "I have a confession to make."

He took a deep breath, then plunged ahead. "Six years ago, out behind Obermeyer's shack, we made a commitment to move to Chicago together to go after our dreams."

Morgan nodded. "I remember. We stayed too long, kissing. I went home to get Christmas Eve dinner started," she said. "And you were going to go pick up Pops for church. Then the sheriff came to the house . . ."

Jesse bit his lip. "That night. Something else happened. After we talked on Christmas Eve, I met with your parents. I told them about our plans. I told them how long we'd been together. And I told them I wanted to marry you before we moved to Chicago."

Morgan drew a quick breath, and his thumb caressed her cheek to calm her. She turned and looked at him, her eyes reflecting her disbelief. "Seriously? You told my mom and dad about us."

Jesse cleared his throat. "Yes. Well. Turns out we weren't very good at hiding our feelings. They knew. Looking back on it now, the only part that surprised them, was how serious we were about each other."

Morgan's lips were tremulous when she spoke. "You told them that . . ."

"We were in love. And wanted to be together forever." Jesse nodded. "Your mom had come prepared. She gave me a small box with a ring inside. Your grandmother's engagement ring. For me to give to you."

Morgan nodded. "It's gorgeous," she recalled from memory. "I haven't seen it in years. A family heirloom. Platinum with an intricate Art Deco setting."

Jesse smiled in agreement. "That's the one. But then . . . well. After your parents died and our plans so obviously changed, I didn't know what to do. I couldn't keep the ring, so I gave it back to Eli—"

"For safekeeping." Morgan confirmed, shaking her head. "When we were cleaning out the house to put it on the market, Eli said he'd put it in a safe-deposit box. I didn't know why."

"I had to share a few secrets with him," Jesse said.

"All these years of hiding and pretending, and the only person I really fooled was myself?" she asked with a grin.

"Pretty much," Jesse said. "Today Eli was waiting for me when I went to catch my flight to Florida. He and Skip gave me a pretty good kick in the pants. Without their guidance, well, I don't know if I would've had the courage to put up a fight and go after what I've always wanted."

Morgan looked out at the tree floating on top of the placid water.

"I'm going to go to commercial pilot training," she said, breaking the peaceful silence. "Skip is going to help me get into the tuition reimbursement program."

"You don't know how glad I am," Jesse said. "I'm sorry I

was less than supportive."

"I'm sure it was a shock."

"I was being selfish last night. I had a picture in my mind of what our future would look like. Then when I heard about you going to flight school, I was angry. I assumed you were delaying our life together again on purpose." He looked up and into her eyes. "So, the tree in the harbor, your beloved tree—in case you didn't already know—it's there to let you know my love is true. It's unconditional. And it's forever. Do what you need to do to make your dreams come true. I will be right here. On Christmas Tree Cove. Waiting for you. Always."

"I hope so." Morgan blinked back her tears. "I can't imagine taking this journey alone. The program is very different now than it was when we talked about it six years ago. So much of it is online. I'll be able to get in my hours and practical experience and still come home on weekends."

Jesse's heart was pounding. "Okay. Now I need to ask you something."

He unzipped his Carhartt jacket and reached inside the top bib of his overalls. Before he had a chance to say another word, Morgan said, "Yes."

"I haven't asked the question yet."

"Yes, please," Morgan repeated. "Go ahead and ask it, but I'm telling you right here and right now, my answer will be the same."

"Will you marry me, Morgan Adair?" He grinned broadly.

"Yes, please, Jesse Taylor."

He opened the little box that held a delicate antique engagement ring, platinum with an intricate Art Deco setting. "My grandma's ring," she said. "It's so beautiful."

Jesse put it on her left hand. Their fingers intertwined. She closed her eyes. When she opened them again, she looked directly into his eyes and said clearly, "I love you, Jesse Taylor. Always have. Always will."

"I love you more," he said. Putting his arms around her, he pulled her in for a warm embrace. He was filled with an endless sense of peace and satisfaction.

She leaned back against him, staring off at the tree floating in the small dinghy called *Hope* in the harbor. "We're going to have to throw another party."

"You have no idea how happy I am to hear you say that." Then he shouted over his shoulder, "She said 'yes.'"

Chapter Twenty-Five

WITHOUT WARNING, THE quiet tranquility of Fish Village was broken. Kayla and Dacey were jumping up and down, hugging each other. Jeff had his hands shoved deep in his pockets. Eli had his iPhone out. Morgan wouldn't find out until later that he'd captured the entire proposal on video.

Within a few minutes, Morgan and Jesse had welcomed an entire party aboard the tug. Pops couldn't stop smiling. Mrs. Kimura brought her gingerbread and passed it around on a tray. Skip was laughing and teasing Jesse. Grace appeared arm in arm with a nice-looking man in a down vest.

This is what her parents would've wanted. All of them— their friends and their family—gathered together. Laughing. Joking. Arguing.

Pops sat down next to her on the foredeck. He took her small hand in his old, gnarled one and held it tightly.

"There's something I've been wanting to tell you," he said. "The night your parents died, the news hit everyone in Fish Village pretty hard. Jesse's dad and I were bereft, until we figured out your dad would've wanted the tree to be floating on Christmas Tree Cove, if only for one last time. So we did it. To honor your parents. And the love they shared."

"Thank you." Morgan had a knot of emotion in her throat. "For honoring them. I'm grateful to finally know the truth."

With her grandmother's engagement ring sparkling on her finger, Morgan was full of Christmas spirit from her fingertips down to her toes. She was surrounded by love. The floating tree had returned to the harbor. All those years wasted. She wouldn't let it happen again.

"We're going to have to do this every year," she said.

"Throw a party on *Faith* in the middle of winter? And invite everyone we know? I'm not sure I'm up for it," Jesse said.

Morgan laughed. "No. The tree on Christmas Tree Cove. It'll our new family Christmas tradition. Something to pass it on to the next generation."

"Yes," Jesse said. "I should almost drown in the harbor every Christmas Eve."

Eli snickered. "It was touch and go for a bit."

"What happened?" Morgan asked.

"I fell in twice." Jesse grinned. His answer made everyone laugh.

"Why didn't you ever learn to swim?" Jeff asked. "You grew up next to a lake."

"I was scared. Of everything and everyone. And I always had Morgan."

"Me?" Morgan looked shocked. "I kept you from learning to swim?"

"Yes. You, you big bully. Always defending me and fighting off my enemies. When you quit on me, I had to learn to stand on my own two feet. I don't know if I would've had the courage to go after what I want." He smiled at her. "What I've always wanted. If only I'd gotten a photograph of your face while you were under the spell of the floating tree."

Morgan smiled. "I still am."

The party went on for almost another hour.

It was after midnight when their friends and family said their goodbyes and wished each other "Merry Christmas." Jesse and Morgan walked down the path to the harbor to get one final glimpse of the floating Christmas tree.

Standing on the dock, Jesse flipped through the images he'd taken earlier on his camera. He stopped when he came to the shots of Morgan walking toward him, her face glowing with happiness, the tree floating on the water over her shoulder. He held the camera at her level so she could see.

"This is the one," he said.

The star on the top of the tree was glowing, brighter and double the size of all the others on the tree, sending out silvery-golden light all the way up to the heavens. Morgan gasped, but said no words.

"That's Christmas magic," Jesse said. "I thought the light at the top of the tree was broken. I nearly drowned trying to fix it. But look. Pop, there it is. Brighter than all the other."

Morgan was certain the eerie glow from the lights on the tree was a message from her mom. Later she'd share the secret with Jesse. Right now, her focus was on his joyful smiling face.

"Which do you love more?" she asked, prompting him as if she didn't know his answer. "All the twinkling stars scattered across the inky black of a midwinter sky? Or the brightly colored lights reflected across the water from the tree on Christmas Tree Cove?"

"You," he said.

She grabbed his chin and pointed his face toward the harbor. "No. Seriously. Look at what's right in front of you with your objective photographer's eye," she insisted.

He covered her hand on his chin with his own and turned back to face her. He leaned forward, and so did she. He rewarded her with a gentle kiss on her soft lips. Shivers of delight followed his touch as she looked up into his face.

"You can ask me every Christmas Eve for the rest of my life, Morgan Adair, and my answer will always be the same." Jesse looked deeply into her eyes. "You. You. It will always be you."

The End

If you enjoyed *On Christmas Tree Cove*, make sure to let others know by leaving a review!

Join Tule Publishing's newsletter for more great reads and weekly deals!

About the Author

Sarah Vance-Tompkins was born in a small town in northern Michigan. She received an MFA in Film Production from the University of Southern California, and went on to work in feature film development for ten years. Prior to film school, she worked as an on-air radio personality. She is a lifetime reader of romance and is excited to be writing in the genre. She and her husband live in Southern California with a glaring of unruly cats.

Thank you for reading

On Christmas Tree Cove

If you enjoyed this book, you can find more from all our great authors at TulePublishing.com, or from your favorite online retailer.

TULE
PUBLISHING